He was unbuttoning his shirt with one hand. Dexterous. Nice fingers. Strong hands. She was silly thinking of that.

Her babies. They'd be premature, susceptible to cold, and this was a cold air-conditioned elevator with a marble floor. And a man's warm jacket. Her babies needed to be warm.

Best place to warm a baby was on the mother's skin.

"I'm a midwife," she said, her shakes finally settling. "Five years in birthing. Skin to skin is my bread and butter."

He smiled into her eyes, his gaze dark swampy green and so very compassionate. "I'm sure you're a wonderful midwife. You'll be an even more wonderful mother."

The wild, spinning world of baby drama stopped for a brief, brilliantly lit, kindness-filled nanosecond. He meant that. If those words weren't the most beautiful thing anyone had said to her in the last month, she didn't know what was. Good that somebody had faith in her.

Dear Reader,

I do hope you enjoy *Father for the Midwife's Twins*.

The twins are so cute but such a lot of work. One of the most amusing parts of writing this book was finding that Lisandra spent a lot of time caring for her babies, as any mother of twins would, and like Lisandra, we both had to find the time to fall in love. A bit like giving a heroine really long hair and you spend a lot of the book brushing and tying it back.

But I wanted that first scene I saw in my mind— Malachi being there in her moment of greatest need.

Lisandra's so capable and independent, and Malachi is such an intense, brooding soul with so much to offer if he could just relax and enjoy life! It had to be a slow-burn and awakening type of love.

I had so much fun as Lisandra coaxed Malachi to show his long-buried sense of humor. It really was an emotional journey for both of them, and I hope you laugh and cry with them as much as I did as they all become a wonderful family.

With warmest good wishes,

Fi xx

FATHER FOR THE MIDWIFE'S TWINS

—

FIONA McARTHUR

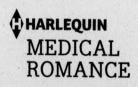

HARLEQUIN

MEDICAL
ROMANCE

HARLEQUIN®
MEDICAL
ROMANCE™

Recycling programs
for this product may
not exist in your area.

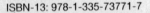

ISBN-13: 978-1-335-73771-7

Father for the Midwife's Twins

For questions and comments about the quality of this book,
please contact us at CustomerService@Harlequin.com.

Harlequin Enterprises ULC
22 Adelaide St. West, 41st Floor
Toronto, Ontario M5H 4E3, Canada
www.Harlequin.com

Printed in U.S.A.

Fiona McArthur is an Australian midwife who lives in the country and loves to dream. Writing medical romance gives Fiona the chance to write about all the wonderful aspects of romance, adventure, medicine and the midwifery she feels so passionate about. When she's not catching babies, Fiona and her husband, Ian, are off to meet new people, see new places and have wonderful adventures. Drop in and say hi at Fiona's website, fionamcarthurauthor.com.

Books by Fiona McArthur

Harlequin Medical Romance

The Midwives of Lighthouse Bay

A Month to Marry the Midwife
Healed by the Midwife's Kiss
The Midwife's Secret Child
Taking a Chance on the Best Man

Christmas in Lyrebird Lake

Midwife's Christmas Proposal
Midwife's Mistletoe Baby

Christmas with Her Ex
Second Chance in Barcelona

Visit the Author Profile page
at Harlequin.com for more titles.

Dedicated to Loretta.

You're a magnificent mother. I'm in awe.
xx The MIL.

PROLOGUE

THE BRIGHT SUNSHINE slipped behind a heavy cloud as Lisandra Calhoun climbed awkwardly from the taxi at her almost-in-laws' house not far from Coolangatta airport. Small splats of rain had begun to fall with increasing force and she didn't have an umbrella. Or a free hand to hold one.

That was okay. It was only water. And she was here.

She'd sent her flight numbers and hoped Josie and Clint would meet her at the airport but they hadn't made it to the terminal by the time she'd picked up her luggage. Josie had said they would. She'd sounded so excited on the phone when they'd arranged for Lisandra to come as soon as she started maternity leave, even before her new house was ready. She'd tried to call but there'd been no answer. Must have been a mix-up, Lisandra had thought—they happened—so she'd caught a taxi.

The flight up from Melbourne had been smooth enough but being seven months pregnant with twins made it awkward and uncomfortable. And she'd been tense with nerves and exhaustion despite the idea of flying from the cold of Victoria up to tropical Queensland. Packing up your life took a toll, though in the end she'd left nearly everything behind to start fresh in the small semi-detached house she'd put a deposit on that was close to Richard's parents. It was a doll of a house, she'd snatched it up as soon as it listed, and despite the long settlement date it had felt right. And there was very little else for sale in the current market.

After the last horrific six months, all she wanted was a safe and secure place for her babies. Despite leaving her Melbourne friends behind, it would be good to be near the only other family her babies would have, and Lisandra would be away from all the bittersweet memories she and Richard had rose-coloured their distant lives with.

At their son's funeral six months ago, a ghastly blur in Lisandra's memory, Richard's mother had said Lisandra should move north, let her help with the baby, and stay with them until she found a place in the Gold Coast. And that had been before Lisandra discovered she was pregnant with Richard's twins and the Smythes would be double grandparents.

She had wanted a change, she thought, as an uneasy foreboding dripped along with the rain down her neck, but she climbed the front steps, dragging her suitcase in noisy bumps upwards. Richard's mother had invited her to come. Had urged her. Lisandra pushed back the disquiet.

It was the right thing to do. Everywhere at home had reminded her of the man she'd lost so painfully, so harshly and horrifically, just a month before their wedding.

Beginning maternity leave had meant sitting at home alone, missing Richard, cradling her bulging belly and waiting for labour to arrive.

No, it felt right to ensure her children knew their grandparents, from the beginning.

Josie would help her settle into her new home when it happened and the boys would know more family than they would have if they'd stayed in Melbourne.

The frosted-glass-panelled door swung open and the sweet face of Richard's mother peered out. Lisandra felt hot tears sting behind her eyes, but she forced them back and smiled. Warm relief eased the cold dampness soaking her neck and shoulders from the rain. She'd lost her parents as a seven-year-old and this woman reminded her of the grandmother who had always been a loving haven for her. 'Josie.' The word puffed out in a little huff of relief.

Josie didn't say anything, instead she glanced over her shoulder back into the house and chewed her lip. 'Lisandra. My dear.' Her hand opened and closed as if she wanted to reach out and couldn't. 'I'm so, so sorry.' She didn't open the door wider.

The rain grew heavier and, even though Lisandra stood under the porch eaves, bouncing water droplets splashed against her legs and soaked her shoes and ankles. It felt as if a yawning chasm had cracked open in a tectonic shift under her feet. Lisandra forced a smile. 'Can I come in?'

The large figure of Richard's father appeared at the door in such a swirl of dark emotion, both Josie and Lisandra stepped back. Josie twisted her hands and disappeared from view, murmuring, 'I'm so glad the cab waited.'

All Lisandra could see then was the twisted

face of Clint Smythe and the wild, frightening grief in the older man's eyes.

'Go away. Get out of my sight. I told Josie, no.'

Lisandra felt the words slap against her. 'What?'

'It's your fault we lost our son. You should have saved him. Your fault.'

The storm of words hit her, like hail, like the lash of rain against her back. She stared aghast into the hard, unyielding, twisted face of Richard's father and knew she'd made a mistake. A huge one. She moistened her suddenly dry lips and tried to make her brain work. 'You're wrong. I tried everything. The paramedics tried.'

'We don't want you.'

She heard Josie gasp and plead behind him but Richard's father went on.

'Get off our property and take your spawn with you. They're not our Richard's babies and you're not foisting them on us.'

CHAPTER ONE

Malachi

'MALACHI MADDEN, YOU are always cancelling dinner. I speak to your secretary on the phone more than I speak to you.' As he listened, Malachi realised he was coming to dislike mobile phones intensely, or at least when Grace rang to complain.

From the fourth floor of The Kirra Beach Maternity Hospital, Dr Madden stared through his office window out over the soothing waves. 'It's a category two emergency caesarean section, Grace.' Which meant he had fifteen minutes to be there.

A hundred metres out from the shore, kite surfers skipped on their boards like bright butterflies from wave to wave with their wind-filled sails. He wondered what that would feel like to be skimming emerald waves in the

wind. Maybe one day, but he knew that scenario looked unlikely.

'Not good enough.' Grace's voice penetrated his distraction with her indignation.
'Your patients always come before me.'

'Well, yes.' *Duh.* 'And patients will be waiting until after I'm finished and that will make
me later. What would you like me to do?'

An odd noise came through the phone.
Could be the sound of gnashing teeth, Malachi guessed. She did that. Funny the things
you learnt about people when you became
more intimate with them. He'd thought he and
Grace were a good idea, mutually low maintenance, when she'd suggested it. His grandmother had seemed moderately excited, but
he suspected that was because she'd given up
on the idea that he'd organise his own love
life.

He imagined she'd hoped Grace would
make an excellent doctor's wife. She wouldn't.
He knew that now. As did Grace. All they had
to do was stop pretending this relationship
was going to work. It wasn't Grace's fault—
he knew he wasn't husband, let alone father,
material, and she had mentioned she wanted
children.

Finally, Grace ground out, 'If you want this

to work you will have to try harder. Get someone else to do the caesarean and share a meal with me on time at least once a week.' Words cold and determined. A finality creeping into her voice. He'd heard that tone before, from girlfriends past.

Get someone else to do the operation? For a patient he'd seen all through her pregnancy? Now something unexpected like an emergency caesarean had arrived and she wanted him to walk away from the mother?

It would be a late night. Unless he was mistaken, Grace was saying choose her over his patients. As well as skip the caesarean for the sake of their relationship.

And here was the answer. 'I can't do that.'

He heard her hiss at his words.

Technically there were half a dozen other obstetricians in the hospital who had asked him to do something similar for them, which he had, but Malachi didn't work like that.

'Then I can't do you,' Grace snapped. 'That's three dinner engagements in the last week. And four last week.'

Malachi wondered who made dinner engagements through the week anyway.

A hint of sadness laced her voice. Only a touch. Mostly, it was annoyance. 'Our farce of a relationship is over. Have your housekeeper pack anything I've left in your flat and I'll arrange to have it picked up.' The call ended.

There was definite relief in the breath he let out.

This was why he didn't do relationships. He was hopeless at them but at the same time he didn't understand how Grace could ask him to hand over one of his clients in her moment of need.

Malachi's brows furrowed as he slipped his mobile phone into his trouser pocket. His father had told him never to ruin the line of the jacket with objects in pockets. As that was one of the few times the old man had actually given him calm advice, he took it on board. His father had been a very, very busy cardiac surgeon. And deeply disappointed in his mild-mannered son.

He pushed his office door wider and stepped into the empty reception area of his office. 'Looks like we'll be running sixty minutes late for the afternoon appointments, Ginny.'

'Yes, Doctor.' His office manager, Ginny, thin, freckled, and happily married, nodded her head.

'I'll come straight back here after Theatre. Please apologise to those waiting.'

Ginny's eyes held warmth and sympathy. 'I will.'

She did apologise really well. Ginny had enough practice apologising for his absence when he was called away to emergencies. She'd probably slip a protein drink onto his desk when he came back, too, because Ginny noticed when he didn't eat. He should give her a rise. He'd get her to arrange it.

Normally, he'd jog up the stairs to Theatres and slip in that way but suddenly he felt weary. Bone weary.

Malachi rolled his tight shoulders and rubbed the dull ache lodged behind the bridge of his nose. Tired. Instead of the stairs he pressed the button for the middle lift. It was coming up and would be quicker.

Of course he felt tired. He'd been up for a breech delivery at three this morning and the Wilson baby's foetal heart rate aberration had given everyone a scare, but it had settled down. At least they'd avoided that caesarean unnecessarily, but he'd had to stay for the birth to make sure, which meant he hadn't made it home before six a.m. And today had been busy all day.

Must be getting old because five years ago he could have done three all-nighters in a row with only a couple of naps. He didn't know why he was surprised that Grace had severed their trial relationship—his father had never been able to maintain a liaison beyond a couple of months, not even the one with Malachi's mother.

Lucky he wasn't planning on kids and having someone rely on him to turn up for parent-teacher night because he'd be hopeless at it.

The lift doors opened and, oddly, the lift bounced a little as it stopped. The inside floor wasn't quite level with the white tiling he stood on. He hesitated. Maybe he wouldn't catch the lift?

He glanced into the small, suspended cubicle. Only one passenger, a blonde woman, and, judging by the voluminous sea-green dress she wore, her pregnancy was advanced. He smiled at her, not really seeing her face, mentally acknowledged the dilemma—he couldn't quite step back and leave her to the odd lift, so he stepped in boldly. Go him. Idiot.

She'd pressed five, the button was the only one glowing, an appointment with an obstetrician obviously, so he'd get out there too and hike up the rest of the stairs.

The lift doors closed and the lift began to jerkily ascend. Malachi put his hand out to the rail at his side and gripped it. Handrails were not something he usually touched, germs and all that, but the cool steel restored his balance.

Up for a few seconds more and the lift

shuddered, bounced once and stopped. It didn't start again. Stuck.

His gaze flicked to the woman across the small space.

'We're okay.' His most composed voice. He looked at the panel and pressed the button again for five. Nothing happened. He tried G for ground. Again nothing. Malachi opened the small door that held the emergency telephone and dialled for the switchboard.

'This is Dr Madden.' His voice unruffled. Matter-of-fact. Yet with authority because he wanted action. 'The central lift has stopped between floors four and five. Please have someone come and release us as quickly as possible. Thank you.' He put the phone back into its cubbyhole and swung the little door shut.

He took out his mobile phone and speed-dialled the operating theatres. 'This is Dr Madden. I'm due in Theatre Three, in five minutes. At the moment, I'm stuck in the middle lift, which seems jammed between floors four and five. I'm sure they'll get us out soon but perhaps a contingency plan for another surgeon for the caesarean might be in order.' He listened. 'Yes. I'll come up as soon as I'm free.'

Malachi slipped the phone back into his pocket and smiled at the woman again.

He held out his hand. 'I'm Malachi.' She didn't answer and he took more notice. She was breathing heavily and holding onto the rail on her side of the lift so tight her knuckles bleached white. Actually, her fingers looked bloodless.

She didn't offer her hand and he realised she had her other palm cupping her belly over her pubic bone. He'd always being quick on the uptake. 'Claustrophobic or in labour?' he asked, his voice gently enquiring. His refrain for life. Even in the face of a screaming woman or an irate bully of a cardiac surgeon. Keep everything composed.

'Not claustrophobic.'

The other then. Labour. Oh. Not too far in labour, he hoped. 'First baby?' They always took longer. Still calm. Feel the serenity.

'Yes.'

He let his breath out but it caught again when she said, 'Twins.'

'Twins.' His brows crept up. Glanced again at the roomy frock. Could be quite far along, too. 'Congratulations. Probably best you don't have them in the lift.' Argh. He couldn't believe he just said that!

She narrowed her eyes at him and he finally

noticed her face. Fine bone structure, a pink bow of a mouth and big eyes the exact colour of the ocean outside his office window. Gorgeous shade. A deep turquoise with flecks of deeper navy. Beautiful eyes.

He was staring. 'Sorry,' he said and blinked to break the spell. 'Stupid thing to say.' And think. 'Lack of sleep, rushing and getting caught in the lift must have scrambled my brains.'

She blew a breath out and he twigged she'd been deep-breathing for a while. 'Regular, painful contractions?'

Her lovely face grimaced as another contraction rolled through her. Gritted out, 'Yes.'

How long had they been here? He glanced at his watch? Less than five minutes. 'How often?'

She didn't answer and he realised she couldn't because she was breathing through the pain in her uterus. Finally, she said, 'Every two minutes.'

Not good. Best to get the information before the next contraction. 'For how long? Who's here with you? And when are you due?'

'The last half an hour.' She looked away. 'Nobody. And not for three weeks.' She sucked in a new breath and he guessed he had about sixtyish seconds to work out what else he needed to know.

He could ask, who should be here with you? Who can I call? Who is your doctor? But she sucked in a gulp and gasped.

Fluid, pink tinged and flecked with white, obviously amniotic in origin, splashed with spectacular force onto the tiled floor of the lift and up the walls in a dramatic wave.

CHAPTER TWO

Lisandra

LISANDRA CALHOUN GASPED. It felt as if someone had just stuck a crochet hook between her
legs and pulled out her bladder.

Except it wasn't an incontinence problem,
it was an Oh-my-heaven-my-babies-are-com-
ing problem. And it was all the fault of the
idiot who said she shouldn't have the babies
in the lift.

Slowly, gingerly, hanging onto the steel rail
with both hands, she eased herself closer to
the floor of the lift and crouched.

The floor looked clean, but couldn't possibly be clean, considering all the shoes that
would have walked all over it. A floor that
was now puddled with amniotic fluid, flecks
of white vernix and tiny stray lanugo baby
hairs. A lift floor where it looked as if, felt
as if, she just might birth when all she'd ever

wanted in life was to create a safe world for her babies. This was not safe!

'Are you okay?' A voice intruded on her panicked introspection. He was crouching down beside her. Shiny shoes and grey suit-trouser legs.

The idiot. She didn't even look at him. 'Of course, I'm not okay.' At least he was a doctor. She'd read about women who birthed their babies by themselves in small places. She hadn't read about anyone having twins in a lift, single-handed, so she'd probably need him.

The idiot rose out of sight and strode back to the telephone cubby and lifted the receiver. 'Escalate the speed of our removal from the lift. There is a woman in labour about to have twins. Get hospital maintenance. They can liaise with the lift company by phone. I want those doors open now.' He put the receiver down.

For some reason the contractions seemed to have paused—hopefully not because she was about to go into second stage and push her premature babies out into this two-metre-by-two-metre marble box.

But, from her half a dozen years as a midwife in birthing suite, she suspected that was a possibility. Transition anxiety. Which could also explain her crabbiness against Dr Malachi Madden. Funny, she remembered his name. Not high on her worry list.

'Sorry.' Her fingers jiggled—great, now she had the shakes—and her voice wobbled as hormones surged. 'I think that was transition.'

'You've done antenatal classes.' He looked vaguely relieved. And unhappy at the same time. Intelligent, dark hazel eyes assessed her. 'You're feeling pressure?'

'Not y…' *No, no, no.* The surge gripped her lower body in an iron fist and squeezed. She grunted. Guttural. Primal. Yanked her dress up and frantically tried to remove her granny pants. Thank goodness for granny pants, she thought wildly as they stretched under her fingers.

Big, gentle hands reached down, holding both of her arms to steady her as she wriggled so, so awkwardly out of her bottom half of underwear. 'Maybe stand when you can,' he said. 'Do the knicker removal properly or they'll trip you up later.'

So, when that urge finished, he hauled her to her feet. She leant on his rock-solid arm and stepped out of her granny pants. If she could care she'd think they'd look so forlorn and embarrassing there on the floor—but she couldn't care. The next pain was coming.

His hand left her for a moment and she desperately missed his support but he was shrugging off his jacket. Tucked it between her feet on the floor and took her arm again.

Ah, she had a clean piece of floor. Thank you. But she didn't have the breath to say it out loud. She leaned into him as the expulsive contraction built.

'Did you want to squat or kneel?'

'Wait.' One word was all she could do. 'Oh!'

She felt something shift down below. And then finally the pressure eased away again yet didn't leave completely. 'I'll squat.' She used to squat as a kid for hours at the waterhole, watching the fish, back on her grandparents' farm before Nan and Pop died. Her safe haven from the world. She wished she were there now.

Malachi said, 'We should get out of the lift soon—but little babies, if they come, they'll need to stay warm. I'll take my shirt off if they birth, not till they arrive, so the material stays warm.'

He was unbuttoning his shirt with one hand. Dextrous. Nice fingers. Strong hands. She was insane thinking of that.

Her babies. They'd be premature, susceptible to cold, and this was a cold, air-conditioned lift, with a marble floor. And a man's warm jacket. Her babies needed to be warm.

Best place to warm a baby was on the mother's skin. 'We can pull my dress off over my head. Pat them over with the bodice that's still dry. I can pull them onto my skin if their umbilical cords are long enough to reach my belly. Put your shirt over the top. K…k…keep them warm.' He looked at her strangely. 'I'm a midwife,' she said her shakes finally settling. 'Five years in birthing. Skin to skin is my bread and butter.'

He smiled into her eyes. His dark swampy green and so very compassionate. 'I'm sure you're a wonderful midwife. You'll be an even more wonderful mother.'

The crazy, spinning world of baby drama stopped for a brief, brilliantly lit, kindness-filled, nanosecond. He meant that. If those words weren't the most beautiful thing anyone had said to her in the last month, she didn't know what was. Good somebody had faith.

A deep, dragging, pulling pain gripped her again and she squeezed his hand as she tried to blow out. No breath-holding. No screaming. Steady slow inbreath and ease that breath out.

'You can do this,' he said quietly with absolute conviction. Yes, she could. But she appreciated the vote of confidence.

There was a thump on the closed doors and they both jumped. The lift jerked. Bounced.

Their eyes met. 'I've got you,' he said and indeed his hand had an excellent grip on hers.

'Let's hope we don't go down together, then,' she muttered and pushed again. There was no stopping this little red wagon her babies were riding on.

On the outside of her very internal world, the lift went up and not down, and when the doors opened, someone rattled a wheelchair in.

Malachi's strong arms scooped her up as if she weighed nothing like a woman pregnant with twins, but she was too busy in her own world to admire his strength. The downward, incredibly powerful urge was on her again.

'Great time to pant if you can,' Malachi said quietly into her ear, his warm breathy tone just for her. She clung to that sanity of connection in a swirling world as the wheelchair spun. 'Just give me one minute and we'll have you somewhere private and safe,' he said.

No. She couldn't. Just one minute was something she didn't think she had.

Gripping the arms of the chair as they sped along, Lisandra jammed her thighs and her mouth as she tried to hold herself together. They were rolling along the corridor at a brisk pace with a small band of noisy people behind her that she couldn't see.

The urge built. She blew breath between pursed lips. Her belly shoved.

A door opened in front of them and she was whisked through but it was too late.

'Now,' she said just as they pulled up beside a bed and she pushed.

'Perfect. You're so clever.' In the distance she could hear Malachi's gentle tones. In that moment of craziness, she clung to that voice.

'Beautiful,' he said as she pushed and then suddenly there was the sound she'd been waiting months for, a crying baby, and a sudden exquisite relief flowed over her in a breath—but that was all the breath she was given.

There wasn't time to relax.

'Now. Again,' she said just as Malachi's arms scooped around her body and softly settled her onto the bed, which she had to admit was easier than arching back and lifting her bottom in a wheelchair. She landed just as the next overpowering surge overcame her.

'I've got you. You're all safe. Let it happen.' Malachi's voice. Malachi's arms. Malachi's hands.

Until a second baby's cry filled the room and she sobbed out the relief at the sound and another sob at the sudden, poignant, emptiness inside her.

So, in the end, Lisandra didn't have the babies in the lift.

Malachi caught them both, smiling up at her after each one, and the babies both screwed their faces and screamed as if someone had taken their favourite toy. And then he disappeared.

Sitting up in the deserted birthing unit an hour later, the staff having rushed off to another emergency, Lisandra blinked around at the tidied room.

At one stage here, the place had looked as if it had been ransacked. Everyone had dashed about expecting the worst-case scenario. She'd given them the best-case scenario—nice, simple, headfirst deliveries for both boys like two tiny seals following each other down a slippery slope.

Who knew she'd be Mother Earth?

Which was lucky because, the twins coming three weeks early, the settlement for her little house wasn't for another fortnight and the contingency plan—Richard's parents' hospitality—had crashed and burned in the worst possible way.

So, she needed to be grateful, because a caesarean section or a horror tear during the births would have slowed her down considerably. Thank you, Malachi Madden, whom she hadn't seen since the births and didn't expect to see again.

After the rushing and the drama had died down a nice young doctor had introduced himself as Dr Cohen, the original OBGYN she'd booked in to see, and said that he would be looking after her.

Thank you, universe, for putting my unflappable Dr Malachi Madden in the lift with me. She'd been relying on the universe a lot, to look after her when Richard's heart had stopped so suddenly, four weeks before their wedding and with their pregnancy just known.

The universe that had helped her find temporary accommodation and kindness with a house-sitting company after Richard's previously delightful parents piled blame on her for not caring well enough for their precious son.

That little flat with the low-maintenance cat she was minding for the travelling owner meant she hadn't been eating too much into her maternity leave pay and the little she made from her online midwifery advice presence.

Sadly, bad luck had found her again. The owner had broken her leg on a ski slope and would arrive home tomorrow. There was no way she could stay in a one-room flat with an invalid, a cat, and two new babies.

Lisandra's new plan would have to be move to a house-share or similar while she waited for settlement and the previous owners of her new home to vacate.

Well… The babies were here. Safely—that was the most important thing. Though, with those moments of sheer terror in a lift before Malachi had stepped in, it had been a close call.

The fact that poor Richard had missed out on all of this made her heart ache. Everything would have been so different if he'd been here with her, but fate had cut him from her life and she would just have to shelve her own heartbreak and do the best that she could with his children.

She wasn't doing so hot with that.

She'd thought moving here had been the best for the children. Just went to show how wrong she could be.

If only she and Richard had had more time, had had the chance of marriage and life together so his father couldn't have disputed her babies were a part of their family, but it wasn't to be. Less than a year together and Richard was gone. Even now, his face in her mind had grown misty without his photo by her bed— but that was only because she had so much else to think about. Once she had her house she'd put his framed face there for recognition in the boys' room and in her own.

All she wanted at this moment was a safe world for her babies. She suspected she'd have to cast herself on the chest of the first social worker the hospital offered to help find a stop-gap until that new home was ready.

CHAPTER THREE

Malachi

MALACHI KEPT SEEING her eyes. Deep pools like the ocean that he could plunge into—if only he had the time. Which he didn't. He'd never been at ease with women. Even the ones who fancied him and put in all the work. He couldn't even keep a convenient woman like Grace happy.

But there was something about Lisandra Calhoun that pierced him all the way to his heart. Stopped his heart. And his brain, apparently, because he was so not the man she needed in her life.

Plus, Lisandra had babies. Babies who deserved a father. A huge fail with him; he hadn't had that training, so it was fortunate for them they weren't his.

Straight after Lisandra's births when the team had taken over, he'd dropped his soaked, bundled jacket someone had given him in a bag off to Ginny, changed shirts and slipped off to the operating theatre to check the mother and baby up there were happy. When he'd apologised for his no show that family's sympathy for his ordeal had made him embarrassed. And thoughtful. Ordeal?

Lisandra hadn't been an ordeal—she'd been a delight. His jacket was sorry, but he had no regret he'd stepped into that wonky lift, though he'd be taking the stairs from now on.

Imagine if she'd been there alone? The thought made him uneasy. Someone should have been with her. She'd said no one was with her but her family should have arrived by now. They'd probably be with her right at this moment.

It had all been just a crazy slice of time where the skills he was passionate about had been useful and appreciated.

With the precipitous babies born so healthy he'd been elated and possibly more relieved than he normally allowed himself to feel. He'd checked with the paediatrician a couple of times when they'd crossed paths, and both boys were with the mother—no need for special care nursery so far—but they were being watched carefully.

He wondered if he should ask his paediatrician friend, Simon, to come in for a second opinion? Shook his head. No, everything was fine with the babies. Hopefully everything was fine with their mother.

Lisandra, who would probably be wrapped in her family's celebrations, should be wearily happy. He hoped so.

It had been a long day for both of them and was nearing eight p.m. now.

Visitors would be leaving.

She'd probably be asleep.

Though, with new twins, he suspected he'd get more sleep than her in the next couple of months. He'd just drop into the midwifes' station and ask how she progressed before he went home.

The midwife smiled at him as he approached the desk. He'd met her a few times. Molly—he'd always been good with names. 'Quick check on Lisandra Calhoun?'

'Lisandra? She's great.' Molly scanned the chart. 'I'm not looking after her this shift, but we all know her. She does an online blog that's super popular with antenatal mums.'

Did she now? Different. And one she could add to after today's experience. 'Has she any visitors with her at the moment?'

The midwife looked at him with an earnest expression on her round face. Almost

pleading. 'No. she's had none except the social worker. Did you know her fiancé died at
the beginning of the pregnancy?'

He knew nothing bar Lisandra's name, par-
ity and delivery date, but he didn't say that.
He shook his head.

Thinking that if he didn't say anything, she
might go on.

Obligingly, her voice lowered to barely a
whisper. 'His parents cut her off—no family support—so if you could suggest to Dr
Cohen to keep her in a couple of extra days
that might help her get sorted.'

Cut her off? Someone was being horrid to
the courageous woman in the lift? That wasn't
right. He narrowed his eyes. 'Is she awake?'

The midwife nodded. 'Yes. This way. The
boys are feeding.'

Molly knocked on a door and pushed it
open. All of the rooms on this floor were single, which was good.

It would be hard to keep two babies quiet
in a shared ward. He was peculiarly satisfied
that Lisandra had comfort and good care, but
he didn't follow down that path of reasoning
about why that pleased him.

Another midwife sat on the edge of the
bed—he knew her, Ris—patting the back
of one of the babies. The other newborn lay

tucked under Lisandra's arm at the breast and seemed to be alert and happy. Not acting prem at all.

'Here's Dr Madden to see you, Lisandra.'

'Hello there,' Malachi said, feeling too much a fraud as a visiting doctor. 'Just a social call before I went home.'

'How lovely.' Her smile warmed and she did look pleased to see him. Some of his awkwardness eased.

Ris stood. 'If it's social we'll give you privacy.' She smiled politely and handed Malachi the infant she'd been patting, which he took because he was fine with them at newborn stage.

As both midwives left, Lisandra called out, 'Thanks, Ris.' Ris smiled and shut the door. Malachi could feel the awkwardness creep over him again.

Funny how he never felt awkward with his patients, but Lisandra wasn't his patient, even though he'd been there for her. Which made him wonder at himself for so adamantly ensuring that the box stating which doctor she was under the care of had been ticked with Dr Cohen, not him.

'How are you?' he said.

At the same time she said, 'Thank you.'

They both stopped and she laughed.

He waved her on. 'Ladies first.'

Her striking blue eyes shone like sequins in a shimmering sea. Suspiciously shiny. Was she crying? Or had she been? The thought pierced him.

'If I'm going first, then, I need to say thank you.' She waved her free hand. She paused as if trying to think of the words until she finally shrugged, smiled and said, 'You are the best person to be stuck in a lift with when in labour.'

Her voice sounded falsely jolly. To him, anyway. But none of his business. None, except it made him sad. 'My absolute pleasure.' He meant it. She looked like a bruised angel with the shadows under her eyes and he wanted to gather her up, hug her to him and protect her. And that wouldn't be happening any time soon. What was he thinking? She'd recently lost the babies' father and been traumatised by a precipitate twin birth. And he was a disaster as a hero. Remaining right where he was, he said instead, 'Do you have names for the boys?'

'Not yet.' She looked at the cots with a soft smile. At the moment, I'm calling them B1 and B2.'

Ah. This he understood. *Bananas in Pyjamas.*' One of his clients had a toddler with two curved dolls and he'd explained the yellow TV characters to him. 'I'm sure more names will come to you.'

She chewed her lip. 'I'm sorry about your jacket.'

He drew his brows together until the thought processed and he remembered the floor of the lift. He waved his hand. 'Good we didn't need it. My secretary sorted that. She's excellent at sorting everything.' Speaking of sorting. He remembered Molly's request. 'You know you can stay as long as you like, here? We can always extend your stay until you're ready to go home.'

Her corn-coloured hair swung as she disagreed. 'Two weeks? I don't think so.'

And there was the prompt. 'Why two weeks?'

She gestured vaguely to the window. 'The little house I'm buying doesn't settle until then. They extended the settlement since I paid the deposit. I hope the sellers aren't wavering.'

'They're probably looking for their own place. Where are you living now?'

'I've been house-sitting a one-bedroom flat. Watering the plants.'

He watched her frown and chew her lip. Surely damaging that petal-pink skin, and he wanted to say, 'Don't do that,' as her teeth chewed down on the soft flesh.

'I've heard of house-sitting,' he offered while his mind tried to imagine her alone in a flat carrying a watering can, but it sounded strenuous for a heavily pregnant woman.

She nodded. 'I was minding the cat, too, but the poor owner's been injured and is coming back now so I'll have to go. It won't hold two babies and the noise they'll make.'

'One bedroom? No. I don't think so.'

'Maybe a hotel for a fortnight if the social worker can't find anywhere else.'

'No family?' It was a reasonable question. Anyone would ask that. Wouldn't they? Now he second-guessed himself. She really did throw him off kilter.

Quietly she answered, 'No family.' She glanced at her mobile phone. 'Can't even ring friends. Mobile phone's dead. No charger. I didn't bring my hospital bag.'

He had the craziest urge to say, I have an apartment that's empty ninety per cent of the time. It has everything. But, of course, he didn't. She'd be embarrassed.

Instead, he stood. 'I'm sorry,' he said again. Useless. 'Stay as long as you like. I'll have a word to Dr Cohen.' He offered her the baby that had gone to sleep in his arms.

She tilted her head at the two tiny beds

on wheels as she lifted the second baby and draped him over her shoulder to burp. 'Would you put B1 in the cot, please? It's easier to have one at a time.'

'I'll bet,' he murmured. Lord, he couldn't imagine how crazy it would get. His world was all for handing them over once they'd arrived. He really had little experience of day-to-day baby care.

He smiled and did as asked, constantly expecting the baby to wake and scream. Inexplicably, the newborn didn't, so he wrapped it in the muslin and tucked it into the cot in the same way he'd watched countless midwives do over the last ten years.

The child stayed asleep. How about that? His hand rested briefly on the little mound of baby and lifted to salute her.

'You were amazing, today, Lisandra.' He smiled and as he walked to the door he said softly under his breath, 'I imagine you're amazing every day.' He turned back. 'Goodnight. I hope you get some sleep.'

'Thank you.' She looked at the corridor past the door and then back at him. 'Will you come tomorrow?'

'If you'd like me to. Of course. But late. To check all is well.' Malachi forced himself to walk away.

* * *

The next evening, this time before seven p.m., not quite as crazy a day for him, he knocked on the door of Lisandra's room and she called, 'Come in.'

She'd intruded on his thoughts many times during the hours since he'd last seen her. And again, at lunch, when he'd bought and brought her a magazine and a cordless phone charger he'd seen in the hospital shop.

She'd taken both gifts without any false protestations. Appreciative but calm. 'Can I pay you the cost?'

'No.'

To his relief she'd just nodded. 'Then, thank you. Wonderful.' The smile she'd given him had made him want to run out and buy six more of each for her, but he'd inclined his head instead.

Now he saw the charger and phone were connected so she'd used it. 'Chargers never go astray.'

'Such a thoughtful gift. And I hated asking the midwives if they'd take my phone and charge it for me.'

He'd thought that, too. Thought about everything. 'You strike me as a person who likes to be independent.'

She furrowed her brows at him but somehow, no idea how, he suspected she was amused. 'You sure that's not just because I'm sitting here alone?'

It was a good question, but no, he doubted he was wrong. Sometimes he read women wrong, look at Grace, but not Lisandra. She'd tell it straight. 'I'm sure.' He said it with conviction.

She smiled. A smile that could energise an army so he felt as if he'd just had a vitamin boost. 'You're a nice man, Dr Madden.'

Dr Madden. Let's not go there. 'Not your doctor, your friend from an extraordinary event, and I introduced myself in the lift as Malachi. You should use it.'

He sat in the visitor's chair. 'How was your day? Did the boys give you a run for your money?'

'Oh, yes. We've had our moments of unusual interest, but I expected that. I sleep when they do.'

Of course she would, which was probably why she looked pale but lovely and not totally washed out. 'You do strike me as a sensible woman.'

Her brows pretended shock again. 'How can you say that? We met with me giving birth in a lift.'

'Ah, but you didn't. You sensibly waited for the birthing room.'

She laughed. 'You're an intelligent man, I can see that.'

'So. They. Say.' He pretended to be ponderous then peered at the babies. 'Have you named them?'

Her shoulders drooped just a little. 'No. Any suggestions?'

He shrugged. 'You could call this one Mal and that one Kai?'

Lisandra snorted. 'What unusual names.'

'But such intelligent names.'

She snorted again, such a funny, cute noise, and they smiled at each other. 'You have a dry sense of humour, don't you?'

'Possibly. Or so all my exes say.' He shrugged. 'Which means I can be a little blunt. I hope you don't mind?'

'Honesty is all I want.'

'Good. Then Molly mentioned your babies' father died unexpectedly. I'm sorry. That must be hard.'

'Yes.' She lifted her lovely chin. 'But even more difficult when I've moved two states thinking his parents wanted the babies near.'

'And they don't?'

Her eyes met his and he could see the hurt, confusion, and, even more sadly, embarrassment as well. 'I thought so. Or I think their grandmother would have made us welcome. But something changed. Accumulated grief, a mental health issue, I'm not sure what happened. But their grandfather basically showed me the door and denied my fiancé was the father.' The words had thickened towards the end. Serious hurt. He wanted to hug her, again, what was with that? He also wanted to snarl at the in-laws.

She said, 'Richard was a beautiful man. I don't understand how his father can be so cruel.'

Malachi would like to have a word with Richard's father. Instead, he said, 'Loss does strange things to people.'

He certainly knew that. His father had become more driven and even colder after Malachi's mother died. 'But you shouldn't be the one to suffer.' There was absolutely no excuse to make her suffer more. 'What about Richard's mother? You say she might have welcomed you?'

A small, delicate shrug, which reminded him she'd had the hugest thirty-six hours and he should leave her to sleep.

Lisandra said after a moment, 'I don't think she has the choice. She texted me to apologise and hoped I found happiness. Asked me not to call. I think that means I can text. I sent her a photo of the boys but didn't ring.'

'Sad.' He agreed. 'But that doesn't help you. Still leaves you out on your own?'

'I'll manage until the house comes through. And I have an online advice business for new mums that will keep me going financially until I go back to work. I do have contacts for work up here.'

'I'm sure you will achieve all you wish. But not yet. Stay and get a routine with the boys.' He thought about the paediatrician and looked more closely at B1. Touched his tiny nose and it turned a pale orange under his finger. 'This young man looks a little yellow.'

'He's sleepier today, too. Hopefully he won't need phototherapy.'

'Probably will. It might take a few days but thirty-seven weeks, a twin, showing yellow already, jaundice is likely.'

'Thanks, Dr Blunt.' But she was smiling, shaking her head ruefully at him. 'Do your patients cry often?'

'Not usually. But then we know each other well by the time they have their baby. They know I'll be there for them.'

'I'm sure you are.'

'I'm here for you, too, Lisandra. I hope you don't mind, but I've asked my secretary to phone your room tomorrow morning. To see if you need anything from the shops. She can pick requests up on her way to work and drop in before she comes to the office. Of course, if you don't answer your phone, she understands you'll be sleeping, but you can text her any needs.' He put a card down on the bedside table. 'Ginny is the kindest person I know and wants to do this. She'll drop by in the morning, anyway, briefly, to introduce herself.'

He stood. Suddenly awkward again. 'Let me know if there's anything else I can do for you. Did someone bring in your suitcase?'

'Molly brought it this morning. The midwives are lovely.'

'They're looking after you. I'm glad.' He moved towards the door. 'Goodnight, Lisandra.'

'Goodnight, Malachi.' He smiled and walked down the corridor towards the stairs. She'd called him Malachi. That made him feel surprisingly good.

CHAPTER FOUR

Lisandra. A week later. Still in hospital.

LISANDRA TOUCHED HER WATCH. Five-thirty. Malachi would be here in an hour or two.

The twins were a week old and as long as she kept their feeds almost simultaneous, she managed enough sleep to feel human, keep herself bathed, and eat. It had been challenging, even with the help of the midwives, but she'd known it would be. But there was delight in the dark blue stares of her boys as they watched her and gratitude in her heart for the precious gifts she'd been given. And sanity in Malachi's and Ginny's visits.

There'd also been a brief 'thank you' text from Josie and a request for more photos when she wasn't busy.

Lisandra was always busy. Luckily B2 was a patient baby and waited with eyes open until his brother was sorted after the feed before having his own bottom changed and being resettled to his cot.

For the last two nights she'd been itching to be out in the world, settling into her new home, finding a routine, reaching for some kind of new normal. But she had to be patient—while being a patient—which was driving her mad.

On the upside she collected amusing incidents for Malachi through the day to share when he arrived but she suspected, with real regret, the tentative friendship that had grown between them might end when she left.

Not that she had time to think about male friends with the boys taking up all of her attention, but she would miss his short and amusing evening visits.

On her first day, she hadn't foreseen visitors over the weekend but he'd arrived at seven p.m. on Saturday and stayed the hour.

On the Sunday night the clock read just before nine, so she hadn't expected him, and she'd been a little emotional with both boys awake and unhappy. Emotional because she'd been tired, not because Malachi hadn't come. Not that.

But when his face appeared around the door she felt as if a load had lifted from her shoulders. Surely coincidence. Again, he'd brought a small gift. A perfect apple and a bottle of exotic flavoured mineral water. Even better, he reached for a grizzling B2 and scooped him up.

She tried for a light voice but her throat felt clogged with tears. 'In the nick of time. He was just about to do his nana.'

Malachi studied her face seriously but his tone stayed light. 'Being B2 that would have been impressive.'

She chuffed a small, unexpected laugh and it felt good. Great even. He was such a life-saver when she needed him—though this was down the smaller end of the scale, she supposed, from looking after her in a lift and in labour.

'Having a cranky baby night?'

'Yes.' She swallowed back the prickling in her throat again. Hormones. It was just hormones and that prevailing tiredness all mothers suffered from. 'B1 is not feeding and they're talking about phototherapy again for his jaundice if his levels go higher.' He'd already had three days of it.

'Better to get it over with,' he said prosaically, and she pretended to frown at him.

'Nice unvarnished truth, thank you.'

'I'll never profess to have the qualities of a good father…' There was something faintly wistful in that statement and it stuck to her thoughts like a grassy thorn to a sock while he went on. 'But I do know my jaundiced babies. This little man will need more phototherapy.'

She believed him. And the way B1 struggled to stay awake for the last feed she was almost ready herself. She watched him with her baby as that first part of his statement niggled. 'Why do you think you wouldn't have the qualities of a good father? You handle these two with skill and assurance.'

'My lifestyle. I'm not present enough for a family. Not my forte.' He waved it away. 'I'll stick with being a busy professional.'

'You're a wonderful doctor, you'd be a wonderful father.'

He frowned at her. As if too polite to disagree but totally doing so. 'I studied from the best to be a doctor...' Then he cut the sentence off and turned to put B2 back in the cot.

There was something here that made her want him to face her, to see what he was thinking if possible, but his shoulders were taut and when he turned his face showed aloof politeness. Not an expression she'd seen before but it said leave well enough alone. Sadly, she didn't. Instead she risked driving him away.

'What do you think makes a good father?'

Black brows rose. 'I have no idea.' He ges-

tured to the cot. 'B2 seems settled. I hope
you get some sleep. You look tired. I'll see
you tomorrow.'

And with that unflattering, though sincere,
comment, he left.

On the Monday Ginny had brought an apple
and two blue hand-embroidered face washers,
a friendly face after only a few days, something she'd sorely needed, along with more
baby wipes.

B1 had become jaundiced again as Malachi
had predicted but the staff returned the portable biliblanket to wrap him, which meant
he didn't have to go under the phototherapy
lights in a cot away from her. Her firstborn
just lived in his bright-lights-on-the-inside
blanket with his eye covers on and slowly
recovered. He'd glowed in the corner of the
room like a little blue glow-worm but today
they'd removed the covering.

So much better than when babies were
taken away from their mother to the nursery
with overhead lights, she'd thought. B2, the
bigger of the two, had avoided the jaundice
and both boys were feeding well today.

It was funny how the naming was becoming such a huge dilemma. Malachi had begun
bringing two silly names on a folded paper,

like Conan and Igor, Panda and Pluto, and even Brick and Diggory. He'd left the papers unopened for her to smile over once he'd gone.

Today was Thursday, she'd finally settled on the boys' names, and they even felt right. That was exciting.

But she was waiting for Malachi. She wanted him to be the first to know. First to hear her decision.

When her phone rang, the ringtone had been turned so soft she barely heard it, but she scrambled to answer. A tiny hope inside wondered if Richard's mother had changed her mind and was coming to visit. Or perhaps it was Ginny with her nightly call. Ginny rang twice a day now. But no, a private number.

Before she could pick it up the call ended after only three rings and she had no way of calling back. Spam, of course. Until the text came in from Beach Realty.

Her heart sank.

Miss Calhoun. It is with regret we inform you that the owner has decided to withdraw his house from sale and your deposit will be returned to you within fourteen days. If something similar comes up we'll contact you.

No. *No.* That was it. All her plans. Her few things in storage. She looked at the time. Pulled the realty number from her contacts and dialled. A recorded message to say they were closed. She doubted the timing was a co-incidence. They were avoiding her. The hoops she'd gone through to secure the loan—something she would have much more difficulty accessing now she was on maternity leave and no current employment—had been mammoth and the thought of doing it all again felt daunting, but she would have to try. Tomorrow. Or the next day. Before she left here, that was for sure.

Her breath hissed out and she stared at the two cots with sleeping babies. All she'd wanted was a safe and stable place for her babies.

The phone in her hand rang again. This time it really was Malachi's secretary. 'Hello, Ginny.' Lisandra's voice sounded shaken, which she was, but suddenly it was too hard not to choke up.

'You okay, Lisandra?'

'Not really.'

'I'm on my way home. Want me to come up and visit?'

'I'll be fine.'

'Of course, you are.' Agreeing. 'But I'll be there in two minutes just to listen.' The phone clicked off.

And that was how Malachi found them half an hour later. Ginny handing tissues to Lisandra and her face a blotchy mess.

Ginny stood when he came in and Lisandra could see the secretary looked relieved. He'd been getting earlier every night since Sunday, she realised. Which was probably just luck but still nice. She sniffed and tried to blot her face.

'I'm glad you're here,' she heard Ginny say, her voice calm. 'Lisandra's new home fell through. The owner withdrew it from sale. Tell her not to worry. I'll get onto finding at least a rental tomorrow when all the real estates are open.'

Malachi's face creased with concern as he stepped closer and touched her arm. 'I'm sorry that's happened to you.' He looked at Ginny. 'That would be excellent.'

'She needs to leave the hospital as well,' Ginny said. 'I was thinking holiday accommodation with washers and driers, and a view to feed babies by, while I work it out.'

Malachi smiled at his secretary and then at Lisandra. 'See. I told you she was good at sorting. Do you have a favourite beach along here?'

Her head spun as she tried to keep up with the conversation. 'I like Kirra. It's quieter than Coolangatta but Coolie is lovely too.' Why hadn't she thought of that? So much easier than a hotel with no facilities in the rooms. Expensive, not as much as a hotel though, and she had savings. Plus, an urgent need right now to get settled. Get her bearings. Start to believe, again, that everything wasn't so bad. She let her shoulders ease back a couple of notches.

'Why not take the loft at my place?' Malachi's words dropped into the silence. 'It's self-contained, soundproof, and you can lock the door between the two sections. Easy.'

Ginny and Lisandra offered him matching stunned faces. 'What?' He frowned at them. 'Just until Ginny sorts you a rental. Seems silly to move until you've found the right place. Even though the loft is part of my apartment I have separate rooms downstairs.'

Lisandra's brain froze. No. Despite how fast a solution to her problem, she couldn't. He didn't know her. Though he had helped her remove her granny pants in extremis, a voice inside whispered. 'No. I couldn't.'

He turned his attention to Ginny. 'It's empty. I trust her. And she's homeless.'

She and Ginny both winced at that. Captain Blunt. Well, she guessed she was, though she didn't like hearing it out loud. But he was right. And there was a gift horse called Malachi staring her in the face. Literally.

Staring into her totally red eyes. 'I want you happy and not weeping with worry.' He shrugged. 'You said all you want is a safe and secure place. I'm not going to throw you out when the boys cry. And it has state-of-the-art security. It's empty. Save the rent for the new place when it comes up.'

His phone beeped and he pulled it out. 'Birthing Unit needs me. Have to go.' He walked back out of the door.

Both she and Ginny stared after him.

'That's Dr Madden for you.' Ginny shook her head fondly. 'He lives at Kirra. It's a two-storey apartment, and the self-contained loft that used to be his father's bolthole to practise his violin is standing empty. There's two bedrooms up there and three downstairs. And Malachi is barely home. That's what Grace said.'

'Grace?'

'Grace was his lady friend. She broke it off

last week. He wouldn't mind me telling you.' She looked at Lisandra's face. 'Don't worry. Neither of them was sorry.'

'I can't move in with him.'

'You're not. It's a separate loft. I've only been there once but I'm pretty sure there was a mini laundry and kitchenette up there as well. The keyed lift opens on that floor, too. Which makes it easy for prams.'

Lisandra put her head in her hands and mumbled, 'How do I say no to all that?'

'You don't.'

When she surfaced Ginny was holding out her hand as if she had all the good reasons in the palm of it. 'Malachi is good people.' She turned up the other hand. 'I think you're good people, too.' She moved both hands like weighing scales. 'He needs a friend. A friend who's a woman would be even better. He doesn't have any that I know of. Lots of acquaintances but he buries himself in work.'

'A friend?'

'Yes. A low-maintenance one—not like Grace.'

'A low-maintenance new mum with twins,' Lisandra said dryly.

Ginny clenched her fist as if catching all those good reasons inside her palm. 'You're emotionally low maintenance. Look at you. You refuse to stay down every time fate tests you.'

'I cried when you came.'

'And then you started working out what to do.' She gestured to the empty doorway Malachi had disappeared through. 'That man is one of the kindest men I know. Despite his sometimes abrupt manner.'

'Like saying I'm homeless.'

Ginny winced again. 'Yep. Like that.' A thoughtful expression crossed Ginny's face. 'He's been less obsessed this week. You and the boys are good for him. He told me once he's never having kids because he can't give them what a father should. So maybe he can learn about himself from you while you're there. Something you can give back to him that he wouldn't get otherwise.'

She couldn't do this. 'It feels so awkward.' She barely knew him. 'He's too generous. I have to pay my way.'

'He won't take it.' Ginny shrugged. 'Just be yourself. Bank what you would have paid for rent and if you ever want to pay him one day—' she shrugged again '—you'll feel like you can. But I'd be keeping it to add to your deposit on a house. He doesn't need the money and would be offended if you offered.' She rolled her eyes theatrically. 'He'd make me figure out something to escape the hassle.'

Despite herself, Lisandra laughed. Then sobered. 'Should I do this?' It was more to herself than Ginny, but the answer came from the other woman.

'Mad if you don't. How about I sort it all for tomorrow after five-thirty? I'll tell my family to buy take-out for dinner on Malachi, and we'll do a girl power move-in.'

CHAPTER FIVE

Malachi

MALACHI SUPPOSED HE'D been pretty high-handed about the suggestion, and probably shouldn't have said Lisandra was homeless, but she was. This was the perfect answer. That said, he'd been happy when the summons from the birthing unit came, so the women could chat about it.

He had full faith in Ginny's good sense and that she'd share it with Lisandra.

With no more waiting for her house there was no reason for Lisandra to stay in hospital. At his home, they didn't need to cross paths if she didn't want to.

Plus, he'd be happy if he knew she was safe upstairs. He had no concerns she'd be a horror tenant nor he a bad landlord.

He'd barely gone upstairs since his father left the place to him in his will so he wouldn't miss it. The old man had soundproofed the loft for violin practice, so he wouldn't even hear the boys if the doors were all shut.

Grace had suggested he renovate, move upstairs and entertain more downstairs, but he'd said he was fine without the entertainment. And hadn't that worked out well? He doubted Grace would have been as welcoming to Lisandra moving in if they were still an item.

All in all, he'd made a lucky escape from a not very convenient relationship there. Though, he probably needed to hint to his grandmother that a woman was moving in and it wasn't Grace. The thought made him smile. She'd be happy for all the wrong reasons but having the one woman he really did care about happy was always good.

By the time he made it back to Lisandra's room it was almost eight p.m. and Ginny had gone. His new tenant-to-be was tucking the boys back into their beds.

He came to stand beside her at the cots looking down at the infants. B2 rolled his eyes and grimaced. He'd probably cry in a minute with wind. 'So? Have you decided if you and the boys will move in upstairs?' He was hoping the conversation wouldn't be awkward.

He should have known better. Lisandra had sorted her thoughts by now.

She snorted. 'You left at a good time. Ginny and I worked it out. Your offer is too good to refuse.' She raised her brows at him. 'Apparently your secretary is going to charge you for take-out for her family and help me move tomorrow afternoon after she finishes work.'

Ah. Good news indeed. 'Excellent.' He tapped the nearest cot gently. 'So, what happened today?'

'Today, I decided on their names.'

Malachi straightened. That was good news. He'd seen the indecision had bothered her but it was something she had to come to on her own. 'Tell me.'

'Bennett and Bastian. B1 will be Bastian and B2 will be Bennett. Alphabetical precedence in age.'

His eyes lit up. 'I like that thought process.'

Malachi repeated the names. 'I like the names. Very masculine and individual. Better than Mal and Kai.'

'I was thinking of those for their middle names.'

She was joking, he thought, but it was a nice story. 'BMC and BKC. That works.' He studied her face. 'Are you ready to leave hospital?' She still looked tired but he could detect that brittle edge women got when they stayed longer than they wanted. He saw that in his work. A lot. Especially when he needed to keep mums in for a complication. Weighing up the medical barrier to discharge with the mother's need to go home and nest.

'Very.'

'Excellent. My housekeeper will put sheets on the bed and stock the cupboards with basics. When you're ready you can order online shopping and they'll deliver anything Mrs Harris hasn't supplied. That's what I do if I want something in. Bachelor perks.'

She lifted her chin and met his eyes. He saw sympathy, thankfully not pity, though he gave Lisandra credit for good sense. 'I'm sorry. Ginny said your relationship ended last week.'

'It was fledgling. Grace and I are both much happier apart.' Her eyes were truly a beautiful shade of blue-green. 'I'm not husband material and it was useful to have that confirmed.'

She frowned at him. 'Perhaps Grace wasn't the right woman for you?'

He shook his head. Shifting uneasily towards the door. 'I prefer to be single. Good-night, Lisandra. Congratulations on the boys' names.'

'Thank you. Goodnight, Malachi.'

CHAPTER SIX

Lisandra

LISANDRA WATCHED HIM GO. Strong shoulders back, head high, powerful legs creating distance between them. He didn't hurry but he moved like an athlete down the hall and didn't look back. Not that he ever did. Always focussed on the next objective was Malachi.

Ginny said he achieved twice as much as other doctors in the hospital and never said no to a request for help.

Lisandra had discovered he didn't like to talk about his personal world but was happy to dissect hers. So, unless he was making personal comments, she'd keep it general, but if he was being personal… She'd ask.

That would be the only way she'd find out what made this man tick. He was turning out to be fascinating, but difficult to understand.

She was still pondering his idea that he

wouldn't make a good father. How much of that was because of his career? What would he even give as his reasons? Maybe he had a ridiculously idealised view of family life—the Hollywood version—home every night at five p.m. Dad was there to play cricket or footy on the weekend, to pick you up from school when you were sick, fun and present and full of dad jokes.

She tried to remember doing things with her father but could only remember him coming home from work and sitting down to tea. There'd been jokes and smiles and she remembered her parents as happy—before they were gone for ever on her seventh birthday. Anyway, now Malachi had stated he wasn't husband material either.

But not any of her business, she reminded herself.

Which was fine.

He would be her landlord. One that wasn't taking any money, which rankled, but she'd do as Ginny suggested and meticulously hoard the payments until she had a chance to pay him back. She had funds.

Obviously, he did too. What sort of apartment had a separate, lockable loft? She suspected it was a very nice one but when she did find a place of her own to rent or hopefully buy, she would move out quickly even if it wasn't as flash as Malachi's.

She needed to consider her little family's long-term future. Malachi might not think he was husband material but he'd find a wife one day and that wife sure as eggs wouldn't want a single woman with twins living upstairs.

And for Lisandra, with twin babies who needed a lot of care, there would be years before any man would be thinking about chatting her up. She wouldn't have the time anyway. In that way both she and Malachi were alike.

When Ris came in to see if she needed anything for the night, Lisandra shared the good news she was finally going home. Tomorrow evening. She'd have to get the address off Ginny for the discharge papers, but she wasn't mentioning to the staff it was Malachi's loft. No offence to dear Ris, but she'd worked in hospitals. He didn't need that sort of rumour running down the halls and seeping like legionnaires' disease through the air conditioners as hot gossip to make people stare at him.

Her staying under his roof was appreciated. It required discretion. And was temporary.

The next evening as Lisandra waited for Ginny to arrive, she'd already taken her few things down to the car park of the hospital and brought back the two little carry seats. One of the things she had achieved in the week before the boys were born had been to have the infant car capsules for the babies installed. Thank goodness for that.

Since last night, online, she'd ordered a twin pram and two porta cots plus all the necessary paraphernalia that went with setting up a baby nursery. All flat-packed and click and collect. All dying to be picked up and assembled. Though she was a little daunted at the idea of assembling furniture and prams between feeds.

She'd planned to collect the purchases on discharge, since she drove an SUV with plenty of hatchback storage area, but this morning Malachi's extremely efficient secretary had suggested she had them delivered. The unopened packages, Ginny assured her, would be waiting for her inside her flat, thanks to the presence of Malachi's housekeeper.

In fact, Lisandra should have her current leftover possessions at the house-sitting flat collected by a courier and delivered. It was only clothes and a suitcase with the baby things she'd begun to gather and her unfortunate hostess had been happy to prepare what was left for the courier. They could pick up her few boxes in storage as well. It wouldn't cost much and save her the hassle.

Lisandra had to admit, after another long day of feeding and caring for the boys, the idea of navigating armfuls of parcels would have been daunting, let alone transferring them from the car park to the unit once they arrived. And to have her few things packed and delivered was just too easy. Bless the woman's brilliance.

A butterfly buzz of excitement fluttered under her ribcage at the thought of having her own space to create the nursery she'd been dying to establish since she'd arrived from Melbourne. She'd refused to buy much until she had her own house, had brought little up the coast as the transfer costs were more expensive than buying new.

But, thanks to Malachi, now she had a short-term haven to relax and nurture her sons. A place of no judgement by others and she could heal from the hurt and distress that had been dealt out by Richard's father.

She still believed the babies' grandmother would one day defy her husband and turn up. So far, she'd only sent one photo of the boys on the day they were born but would send another today. Intending, unless she was asked to stop, to send one a week for the first four weeks and, if she still had no reply, then one a month for the first year. It broke her heart she didn't have a photo of Richard as a baby so she could compare with the boys. But she suspected Josie was suffering, too. When she was out and about, she'd make two matching baby photo albums—and keep one for Richard's mother. Perhaps one day she would hear from her.

For now, she had her new life to get on with. She wouldn't be lonely. Malachi would drop in after work every now and then to catch up with the latest news of the babies. But even if he didn't, she knew downstairs, or with Ginny's contact number, someone cared about them, and would be there in an emergency. There was a lot of peace in that thought and she would be grateful to Malachi Madden and his secretary for ever for that gift.

Ginny arrived and suddenly, in a flurry of goodbyes to the staff, she was in the lift with Bennett and Bastian and Ginny. Going home with twins.

In the same lift they'd nearly arrived in.

Funny how the memory didn't bother her. She and Malachi had managed. She'd apparently been sensible, as Malachi said, but the maintenance people getting the doors open had allowed that boon.

Holding one baby capsule and her hand-bag, she looked at the corner where a week ago Malachi had laid down his suit jacket and crouched beside her.

Lisandra's lips twitched and she shook her head with a smile at the memory. She almost wished he'd been there to meet her eyes and share the moment. But that was silly. He probably thought of it as a disaster that hadn't quite happened.

Once the boys' capsules were loaded into their safety-locked cradles, she followed Ginny's car in her own to the boom gate. Lisandra slipped into the fast-moving traffic for the first time in a week and she had a sudden crazy feeling of panic.

What if she had an accident with the boys in the car?

What if she died suddenly as their dad had and the boys were left alone in the unit?

Lisandra crushed the feeling down. She would manage. She would manage it all. But for the moment, Ginny and Malachi were there. She had friends. She and the boys weren't alone. That fact was priceless.

The indicator light from the car ahead brought her back to the present and she followed Ginny left down another boom-gated car-park ramp. She tapped the electronic key card she'd been given to keep the boom gate up.

Ginny had told her Malachi had two car-parking spaces and Ginny would park in the visitor's parking. Ginny stopped and indicated a parking spot directly opposite the lift doors next to a long, low black sports car with chrome spoked wheels. She'd never been a car buff but it looked fast and expensive and she'd have to be very careful when she opened her doors not to scratch it.

She'd certainly moved into a privileged position and even though she hadn't had time to look at the outside of the building very much, she'd seen the beach opposite, and the cars surrounding her looked like a private school of automobiles.

She shrugged and tried not to be excited. This was lovely holiday accommodation until she found her for-ever home for the boys. But very nice for a brief sojourn.

When she opened her car door Malachi stood with his back against the sports car next to her. She blinked. 'Malachi?'

'I finished early. I thought I'd come and see how you settle in.'

'Oh. Thank you.' A well of delight and happiness surged up her chest and into her smile. 'How lovely.'

His eyes widened, and the smile he gave her back held a tinge of shyness. 'I'm glad. Though I can't guarantee I won't get called away, so we'll still ask Ginny to stay. I was thinking about the parcels Ginny mentioned and I've always loved assembly puzzles. Maybe I can help?'

'Excellent,' she said, trying to damp down her pleasure. 'I dislike building them intensely.'

When they were standing in the lift with Ginny, nobody spoke as the floor lights blinked past and Lisandra thought about that day a week ago when she met the man standing so still and tall beside her.

He held Bastian's carry cot. 'Were you nervous getting back in a lift?' He must have been thinking of it too.

Lisandra smiled. 'No. And it was the same lift.'

'Oh, my heaven, I never thought of that.' Ginny looked horrified she hadn't been supportive. She turned her head and stared at Malachi as if surprised he had.

Why was Ginny surprised? Malachi was always thoughtful. Lisandra shook her head. 'I have no bad memories from that day. Once

Malachi stepped in I knew I had help even if I did have the babies. When it jammed—' she shrugged '—he was so calm about ordering them to get us out I knew he had that part under control.'

'Glad I fooled you, then,' Malachi said dryly.

She grinned at him. 'And he didn't seem fazed when my waters broke all over the floor.'

Ginny made a strangled hiccough of a noise. 'He doesn't get fazed.' Ginny looked at her boss fondly. 'A furrowed brow is all you'll get as he works on the solution.'

They both looked at Malachi, who shrugged. 'No idea what you two are going on about.'

Lisandra smiled again. Said softly to Ginny, 'Yes. I was lucky he stepped in.'

'Maybe you both were,' Ginny said even more quietly as the lift doors opened right at the last number, but Lisandra stared at Malachi with wide eyes. 'Do you have the penthouse?'

Malachi shrugged. 'Inherited from my father. I enjoy the view.'

'I thought you knew that.' Ginny grinned. 'Penthouses are the only apartments I know with lofts. Just enjoy it.'

Her cheeks had grown hot at the idea of the

luxury, but she suspected she would 'enjoy' living here indeed.

Lisandra looked down at Bennett in his little capsule. Sang very softly to him about going on a summer holiday. Ginny laughed. Malachi looked intrigued and she stopped in embarrassment. Then she looked at the small entry and closed loft door.

She turned to Malachi. 'Would you like to show me?'

He gestured with his hand inviting her to precede him and they stepped out into a foyer each carrying a car-seat capsule with the boys asleep. Bonus, right there. Much more fun when the babies weren't screaming.

He swiped the door lock. 'The lift to here isn't accessible to floors below mine, unless somebody has our code on their card. People such as maintenance and reception do. I'll keep mine in case of emergencies but won't use it without your permission.'

'Thank you.' What else could she say? Especially in view of her earlier dire thoughts, it was good he had the back-up access.

The door swung open and white marble tiles flowed from the front door through the serene lounge area to the narrow, wrap-around balcony. Straight ahead blue waves and blue sky stretched across the Tasman Sea, technically all the way to New Zealand.

Loft? It looked like an enormous open-plan house on the top of the world. 'So much bigger,' she murmured. Good grief, she'd arrived at the Taj Mahal.

Malachi made a small, pleased sound, as if happy she liked it. She raised her brows at him. Who wouldn't? 'Downstairs is much larger and there's a small private pool.' His tone was amused. 'The boys might be a bit young for that, but you're welcome to use it.'

No way in heck was she sauntering through his house to get to his pool.

As if he'd read her thoughts, he said quietly, 'There's a spiral staircase off your veranda down to the pool.'

She raised her brows. Snorted. Couldn't help herself. 'Of course, there is.'

He looked pleased. 'You find it over the top, too?'

She laughed. So, it seemed extravagant to him as well? That was interesting. 'Yes, Malachi. But wonderful.' More seriously, 'Thank you for trusting us into your home. I won't take advantage of your kindness.'

'I know that.' He shrugged. 'Nobody else uses it. And that's your internal stairway down to my apartment if you need me in an emergency. The lock is push button and on your side. Of course, I have a key, but won't use it unless you need me to.'

If she locked herself out? Or in an emergency? She prayed that would never be required and turned away from the thought of something so bad she'd run to Malachi. She turned her face to the room.

Thick blue rugs lay between two long white leather sofas, with blue shell-embroidered cushions and white occasional tables and lamps. Not cluttered, but soothing and seamless leading to open floor-to-ceiling doors and the narrow wrap-around balcony twelve floors from the ground. Thankfully, glass enclosed the drop from over waist height. Not that she'd still be here when the boys were crawling, but still. That was some drop.

They stepped in further and he pointed to a white door to the left. 'Butler's pantry in there with sink, coffee machine, small stove and microwave.'

Then to another door next to it. 'Guest bathroom and laundry. The boys' room, and your room at the far left with en-suite bathroom.

Malachi crossed the wide living area to the external glass doors and opened them to the gentle ocean breeze carrying the tang of salt, and the sound of distant waves and seagulls. Lisandra put her carry cot down and followed him.

The bay curved away in both directions, left to Surfers Paradise in the distance and right, back towards Coolangatta and the Tweed, though she couldn't see around the headland. Curving footpaths butted the beach and swept under trees and palms in both directions. Utopia for anyone...let alone a new mother with twins. 'Plenty of places to push a pram down there,' she said.

'Are you going to have the boys in with you tonight or in their own room?' Malachi asked.

'I think I'll keep them with me for now, until I'm used to sleeping here. But I can't wait to set up their things.'

'Let's do that, then.' His eyes gleamed. 'If I start with the pram assembly you could put them there for the night and just push them around the loft.'

She looked at this tall, gorgeous, generous man offering his time, a precious commodity he didn't have much of, with such enthusiasm. 'Are you a thwarted engineer?'

'Apparently,' he said over his shoulder as he headed to the butler's pantry. 'There should be a knife in here to open the tape.'

She exchanged looks with Ginny, who

shrugged. 'I hate assembling,' she said, and gestured to the suitcase.

Lisandra nodded. 'Me, too.'

Two hours later Lisandra stood beside Ginny waiting for the lift. Her new friend had been busy. She'd sorted the boys' new clothes, wraps and cot sheets and washed them in the pure soap she'd brought for just that purpose. Those that could be whirled inside the clothes dryer in the guest bathroom were either dry or still doing so and those that couldn't stand the heat had been stretched on the clothes-drying rack that pulled out from the bathroom wall.

Ginny screwed her face. 'You sure you don't want me to stay until all the clothes are dry? I can fold them and put them away in the wardrobe.'

Lisandra shook her head. 'You've done enough. Took the biggest load off me while I've just sat on the lounge and fed the boys. The least I can do is fold some clothes.'

Ginny looked back in towards the boys' room. 'It's all worked out really well.' Her gaze travelled over the pram that sat next to the lounge with the two boys asleep in it. 'So good Malachi managed as much as he did before he left.'

Malachi had assembled the pram, while

Lisandra fed the boys, and Ginny made it up for them to sleep in. Malachi took himself into the bedroom to assemble the change table and the portable cots. Five minutes after he was done his phone rang and he left to return to the hospital.

All around her those two wonderful people had unpacked and sorted for her and by the time she'd resettled the boys after the feed—everything was done.

Thank you.' Lisandra leaned forward and hugged her. 'You're a champion, Ginny.'

'You'll be busy enough while you ease these boys into a routine. I think you're the champion. Having one baby at a time was hard enough for me, and the last was sixteen years ago—I still remember the exhaustion. Watching you juggle the two of them fills me with awe.'

'Thanks to you and Malachi I don't have anything else to do. I've been given a beautiful place to stay and now you've organised everything else. I'm feeling very spoiled.'

'You sure you don't want me to make you some food before I go?'

Lisandra shook her head. 'Go home to your family. The boys are asleep. It's my first night with them and I'm excited. I'll just have something simple.'

The lift arrived and Lisandra waved at her new friend as the doors shut.

And then she was alone. Just her and the boys in their new home. Suddenly the space was silent except for the swish of the waves in the distance and the traffic far below.

When she stepped out onto the balcony the crescent moon hung over the ocean leaving a trail of sparkling light across the waves. Across the bay, the night-lit buildings of Surfers Paradise twinkled in the distance.

She walked to the end where the small, gated spiral staircase led down to the floor below. She could just see the edges of the pool with the blue of the water lights glowing under the surface.

She turned and walked back to the other end of the balcony and stared out along the beach far below. It was going to be very hard to return to ground level once this little holiday was over.

That was what it was, though, a holiday for her and the boys to get used to each other. She was blessed at the opportunity and wasn't in a position to be squeamish over the favour she'd been given as a gift beyond expectation. Somehow, she'd figure out how to repay Malachi, but for tonight she'd just soak it in.

CHAPTER SEVEN

Malachi

ON SATURDAY MORNING before Malachi's alarm went off, he lay on his back smiling at the ceiling, still enjoying that pleasure of accomplishment from yesterday. Lisandra and her babies were settled upstairs. Strange how good that made him feel.

He hadn't heard any noise at all and hoped Lisandra realised that she didn't have to worry about disturbing him. Next time he saw her he'd remind her of that.

The alarm beeped quietly and he rose, dressed, and left to jog along the shoreline from headland to headland, the best part of living at the beach, and even if some mornings he was called out, that only made the dawns he did see more satisfying.

Grace had not been an early riser and hadn't appreciated him disturbing her as he dressed for his run. All in all, life was so much simpler and more pleasant without Grace, which reminded him he needed to let his grandmother know he was not headed for a long-term relationship.

He'd been a fool to expect any relationship to not be a rolling disaster—but the few times he'd suggested it might not be working Grace had managed to reassure him until he'd been distracted by work. Luckily, even work had finally exasperated Grace.

Today, he'd invite his grandmother over and break the news. If it all worked out she could meet Lisandra and the twins before she formed the wrong idea.

Malachi had only been back from his run for half an hour when his doorbell rang.

When he swung open the door he was expecting Lisandra, actually, hoping for Lisandra, as only one other person had a key to his level, but it was a tall, grim-visaged woman, who lifted her chin at him. He should never have given Gran a key, but they'd both agreed asking Reception to be allowed to visit her own grandson was unacceptable. But she always knocked.

Busted. Too late. Millicent Charles, his mother's mother, stood almost to Malachi's height. His gran had never suffered fools and he'd been a clown not keeping her up to date. She didn't intimidate him, the thought made him smile, but he indulged her because she deserved some indulgence from someone and he was all she had.

'Grace tells me your relationship has ceased to be—just over a week ago.' She looked him up and down. Not impressed, her narrowed eyes said.

'Please come in, Gran.'

'Thank you,' her cultured voice clipped as she swept past. Seemed he had some explaining to do. His mouth kinked up. He loved her very much, but she would be cross.

More proof of her displeasure came his way. 'One would have thought one's grandson would have mentioned that fact.'

'Grace didn't appreciate my current workload.'

'What woman would?'

Lisandra didn't seem to mind. 'My apologies. I intended to invite you for lunch to speak to you today.'

'Too late. I'm here. You could make me coffee if you're not dashing out.'

'Love to.' He held up his hands peaceably. 'I'm not going anywhere.'

'Unless your silly phone rings.' His grandmother knew him well.

'My phone is quite clever but I'm not on call either,' he said mildly. 'Would you like something from the patisserie?'

'A dreadful frozen something?'

'Fresh this morning after my run.'

Millicent appeared slightly mollified. 'I might.' She glanced towards the balcony. 'I'll sit out on the deck and wait for you. I always did appreciate this view.'

Malachi cast his own look towards the wide-open space of the outdoor entertainment area. All he needed now was Lisandra to be spotted upstairs by his grandmother before he could ease into the fact that he had a stranger and her newborn twins living above him.

Of course, it was his house, he could invite whom he wished, but he didn't like to upset Gran or give her the wrong idea. She had that dicky heart and was the one person who had loved him unconditionally when his world fell apart. He knew she wanted him to be happy but he didn't need her assuming Lisandra was his new girlfriend. She'd be embarrassed at her mistake. To make his guilt worse, Ginny had reminded him twice yesterday to ring his grandmother, but both times he'd been called away before acting on her advice.

Last night, it had been too late coming home from the hospital after his call back, and he'd been busy enjoying that warm sense of accomplishment thinking of Lisandra relaxed and happy with her babies. He'd had an amusing time assembling the pram, the change table and setting up the little portable cots. The uninhabited loft had taken on a heart and soul that had been dreadfully lacking in the space before.

He'd known it was too late to go up and see them then but knowing she'd been up there with her babies had left him strangely content.

Now he had to explain that to his favourite, and only, relative without sounding like an idiot hoodwinked by a beautiful woman. He knew it wasn't so. And when his grandmother actually met Lisandra, she would know the same. Still. A difficult conversation that didn't need an interruption by a crying baby above.

Which was exactly what the distinctive newborn wail drifting in through the open doors provided. His lips twitched. Oh, dear.

Malachi put his head down, smiling, and prepared his grandmother's latte the way she liked it and then his own long black coffee. Next, he placed a pastry on each of two small bone-china plates along with paper napkins. A skill she'd insisted he learn when he'd spent his weekends with her in his teens. She'd grumble about the lack of linen but he expected there would be more to discuss than that.

Everything went on the tray and he carried it out to the long outdoor table under the shaded area. He didn't glance up.

When he was seated and the tray had been distributed, he said, 'In more news…'

'You have a woman living upstairs with a baby?' his grandmother said dryly.

'Yes. Lisandra Calhoun. With newborn twins, actually. I'm sure you'll like her.'

For once it seemed Malachi had silenced even his grandmother. He let the pause linger as she assimilated his words for just the right amount of time before she could assemble a question.

'We've become friends and the house she was buying fell through so I offered her the loft.' He shrugged. 'Basically, I'm her landlord.'

There. That sounded very reasonable and sensible. She couldn't have any problem with that.

'So, you are charging her rent?'

Malachi frowned. He didn't need money. 'No.' He lifted his brows. 'Why would I?'

'It's what landlords do.' Millicent sipped her latte.

'Not this one.'

'I see,' his grandmother said.

'I'm glad,' he said and smiled at her. There you go then. All done. 'How have you been, Gran?'

'Oh, no, you don't, Malachi Madden. I want to hear the rest of the story.' She lifted her own chin.

'No more to tell.' He shrugged. 'Lisandra was looking for a place to rent short term and upstairs was empty.'

'I heard that bit,' Millicent murmured, her tone deceptively soft. 'I want to hear the section about where you met her and why have I never heard of this friend before.' She pressed her pastry with one manicured fingernail and, apparently satisfied, lifted it, pausing before it reached her lips. 'And, how it is that you trust her to move into your life like this.' Her gaze drilled into his and behind the imperiousness he saw concern. For him. Real worry. No need for that.

Somehow, he deduced the fact that saying he'd known Lisandra for only a week wouldn't go over well. Malachi thought about what he wanted to tell his grandmother and what he didn't. He thought about how much she'd been there for him in the times when no one else had been and the fact that he knew she cared for him very much. This consideration was followed by his natural aversion to raised voices.

'I like Lisandra better than Grace.'

'I'm not sure that's a compliment,' Millicent said, 'since I didn't like Grace.'

He blinked. 'You never said.' And if she had, maybe he would have put that with his own doubts and bailed much earlier. 'I thought you liked her.'

'I was happy you were in a relationship. Not so much with Grace. I could see Grace was more of a casual partner and I accepted her assurance that if you did eventually become a couple she'd be securing an heir for the future. There will be a fortune you and I will leave behind.'

'Oh.' Grace had mentioned children.

'Is this woman going to step into her shoes?'

'No.' The word came out more forcibly than he intended. 'Lisandra is a friend.' Surprisingly, that too was true. 'A good friend.' Or at least he hoped so. 'There are no ulterior motives for Lisandra being upstairs and she will go when she's ready.'

He picked up his own pastry. 'Perhaps now, we could go back to my original question—

how are you, Gran?' He opened his mouth and took a big, it-would-take-a-very-long-time-to-chew bite.

'I'm well.' In the distance a baby cried again and Millicent glanced up, but of course the shade sail blocked her view. 'How is she managing with twins on her own?'

Eventually he swallowed. 'Well. She is a very sensible woman. And a midwife, so she has skills.'

'And will I meet her?'

Malachi gave up. The sooner the better probably.

'I have no idea how her day is progressing, but I can certainly phone her and ask if she would like to join us.'

CHAPTER EIGHT

Lisandra

LISANDRA'S PHONE RANG as she pushed the pram towards the butler's pantry. If she had only two small coffees a day, it didn't seem to disturb the boys and she'd been dying to try out the new coffee machine in the nook.

Sometimes, over the last week, there'd been a few times when she'd felt everything was out of control but now moving into Malachi's loft she had a stable base to build on. So it wasn't surprising she felt more in control.

She didn't recognise the number. Which explained the question in her voice when she said, 'Lisandra?'

'Good morning. It's Malachi.' The usual calm thrum of basso she'd grown to admire so much made her smile. Gave her a little thrill, actually. Something she hadn't expected to happen—was she that kind of fool? Hadn't she had enough heartbreak?

Here she was, excited because he'd phoned, though perhaps it was just because she didn't have his number, the emergency thing had worried her. That was the only reason.

Really? Mmm-hmm? Liar.

That thought swiftly followed by a stab of guilt that Richard, someone she'd loved so much that they'd been set to marry and spend their lives together, had been dead less than a year—and here she couldn't deny she felt drawn to a man she barely knew. Kindness. It was only the kindness. But she suspected she was lying to herself.

'You still there?' His deep voice bringing her back to the present.

'Oh, yes, sorry.'

He asked, 'How are you?'

'Human. Thank you. And happy waking up in this lovely place, Malachi. I hope you weren't too late home?'

'Not long after ten.' She could almost see the shrug. The man worked ridiculous hours but it was none of her business.

'How are the boys?'

'Good. Seems they enjoy sleeping in the pram. I've just popped them back in. I was looking at your new coffee machine, considering giving it a go.'

'Perfect timing. Would you consider pushing the pram into the lift and I'll make you one down here? My grandmother has popped in and would love to meet you.'

His grandmother. Oh, I'm sure she would, Lisandra thought with an uneasy wince as her neck tightened. She couldn't help thinking of Richard's father's horrid accusations. What would Malachi's grandmother think? Or say?

When she didn't answer immediately, he said, 'Or you can leave it and join us for lunch if that works. Or another day. No pressure.'

No pressure. Right. If she'd been Malachi's grandmother, she'd be wanting to know who the bird upstairs with the babies was, too.

Lisandra glanced down at her new stretch jeans and button-up shirt, which, she had to admit, she'd put on in case Malachi dropped in. 'Meeting your grandmother, as well as coffee I don't have to make, sounds perfect. Give me five minutes and I'll be at your door with my pram. We can hope they sleep.'

'Perfect. Sorry about the short notice.'

'That's fine. Good practice.'

'I have pastries from the patisserie.'

Just what she needed. 'The last thing I need with twin baby fat.' Then felt like an idiot because she imagined he'd heard that many times before in his job.

'Good,' he said, and she wasn't sure if he meant because he got to eat all the pastries or because she was coming, but she could hear the smile in his voice. Then the call ended abruptly in a typically Malachi way and she slipped the phone into her pocket.

'Bye,' she said to the closed connection.

Lisandra backed out of the pantry and glanced at the boys both sleeping. One little capsule in front of the other with Bastian's higher at the back and his brother's closer to her. She appreciated the design because she could see both their faces. 'Our first excursion in your new pram coming up,' she said to the sleeping babies. She spun and hurried into her bedroom to brush on a touch of lip gloss and sweep a comb through her hair. Before the boys woke.

Her clothes would be fine for his grandmother, she decided. It would be worse to dress up for coffee when everyone knew she'd planned to be at home.

She had nothing to be nervous about but that didn't stop the wriggling in her belly and the slight increase in the rate of her breathing.

If Malachi's grandmother was anything like him, she'd be very proper and straightforward.

And perhaps silently horrified at her grand-son's philanthropy.

Oh, well, no use worrying about something before it happened. At least he hadn't brought his visitor up here in the middle of a feed.

Two minutes later, waiting for the lift doors to open, she couldn't decide if she wanted to push in frontways with the pram or back in for a smooth exit. Backing in seemed the most sensible thing, especially when the lift was empty, so she tried that. All new adventures she had in store.

When the lift stopped one floor down, Mal-achi's door had been chocked open. He must have been listening for the ding of her arrival, because he appeared almost immediately.

'Hello.' His dark hazel eyes were warm and welcoming, and she felt her own mood lift. 'How are you managing with the pram?'

'It's a work in progress.'

'Excellent.' An appreciative smile this time. 'Good we don't have steps to traverse.'

'True story.' When she stepped into his apartment it seemed to stretch twice as far as hers, probably because the sea air flowed seamlessly through open sliding doors to the wide terrace instead of a narrow balcony. The same white marble expanse, more white and blue accents, on a much grander scale, with a wall-length television screen and a small, curved bar with stools. An eye-boggling array of spirits that could have stocked a wild west saloon made her blink and she looked at Malachi.

He must have been watching her face because he nodded. 'My father's bar. Seemed a shame to toss them. I rarely drink.'

He wouldn't have opportunity, which was why she'd been surprised. He'd always be climbing into the car on his way to the hospital.

'Your home is beautiful.' She gestured at the enormous room that seemed to stretch in all directions.

'It's too big for one man. Push the boys over near the lounge. We'll hear them from there.'

Once she'd done that, and the brakes were on, he gestured her out of the doors. 'Come through and meet my grandmother, Millicent.' There was an underlying gentle pride when he said grandmother, and she could see he was fond of her. That was sweet. 'She and your coffee are waiting.'

She smiled at him. 'I look forward to meeting her.' And she actually did look forward to learning more about his family.

A tall woman, possibly early eighties, stepped away from the balcony rail she held and turned their way. Not quite as tall as Malachi, wearing silk jade trousers and a paler green, almost white sleeveless tunic, the silk pantsuit softly draping her reed-thin body. Her make-up glowed with perfection and her short, curly, snow-white hair sat artfully tousled. Her smile appeared pleasant but inscrutable.

'Gran, I'd like you to meet Lisandra Calhoun. Lisandra, my grandmother, Millicent Charles.' So, probably his mother's mother.

Lisandra smiled. 'It's lovely to meet you, Mrs Charles.'

The actually quite scary lady smiled back. 'Likewise. And, please, call me Millicent.'

'Thank you.'

She inclined her head towards the pram through the doors. 'Malachi says you have twins. What did you call them?'

Lisandra glanced at Malachi and then back towards the still silent pram. Their eyes met and the history of the names flashed between them. 'Bastian and Bennett.' She didn't add the Mal and Kai that sat in the middle of their monikers.

'Bastian and Bennett Calhoun.' Millicent's amusement flowed to her eyes, which had warmed to the same hazel as Malachi's. 'Two very auspicious names.'

'Yes,' Lisandra said. 'They are. Would you like to see them? They're asleep, which in these early days is a bonus.'

'Of course.' So, they all trooped in and looked down at the sleeping babies. Bastian wrinkled his nose with a dream and Bennett pursed his lips and made a kissing noise. She adored them both so much it was almost overwhelming. When she looked up Malachi was watching her with an intense scrutiny and something that looked almost like wonder.

He said quietly, 'I think they've changed and grown in just one day. Are you getting sleep?'

'I wouldn't be surprised if they've grown. As for sleep…' she shrugged '…enough.'

When she looked towards Millicent she was watching both of them, not the babies. 'Very handsome young men. I think they look a little like you.' Her gaze swung away from the pram. 'They're a credit to you. I can see you're an organised mother. Before they wake up you deserve one of Malachi's excellent coffees.' She smiled and turned to go back towards the terrace.

Once they were all seated again at the glass table Lisandra sipped her latte and sank back in her seat. Oh, my goodness, she'd needed that coffee. She smiled at Millicent. 'You're right. Malachi makes excellent coffee.'

'You must be very busy up there.' The older woman raised her eyes to the ceiling.

'I'm rushing a little too much if I want to get something done, at the moment.' She shrugged. 'Like heading to the shower. I need to achieve that while they're asleep.' She shook her head. 'It's as if one senses the other is awake and doesn't want to miss out on anything.'

'That sounds like children, men in general, really,' Millicent said dryly, 'but tell me…' She paused, and Lisandra knew what was coming. Just knew. 'Where did you meet Malachi?'

And how much did she tell? 'In the hospital,' she said.

'Of course,' Malachi broke in, 'Lisandra was not my patient.'

His grandmother glanced at him. 'Of course, my darling, you are nothing if not professional.'

And Lisandra wondered why she hadn't thought of that complication. Had Malachi left himself open to censure?

'We met in the lift.' Lisandra glanced across at the man who had been there for one of her more terrifying moments.

His eyes were on her, warm and there was amusement crinkled in the corners. When she looked away, and back at his grandmother's face, she appeared intent on them both.

'I was already in the lift, Malachi stepped in, and the lift jammed. My waters broke. It was messy.'

Millicent's eyes went wide. 'Disconcerting,' she said. 'How many people were in the lift?'

'Just the two of us. Malachi remained completely calm.'

As for the idea there could have been others? Not a pleasant thought. 'I hadn't really thought about others. I guess I was lucky.' She couldn't imagine a whole roomful of people with damp shoes and she winced at Malachi.

'Not really worth thinking about.' He waved his hand. 'So best not to.'

She shook her head at his practical statement.

Millicent raised her brows. 'Did you have the babies in the lift?'

'No. Despite the fact the lift stayed jammed. We were rescued in time.'

'I told you she was a sensible woman.'

'You did. This does become more and more interesting,' his grandmother said as she lifted her cup and peered at them over the top of the rim. Her eyes sparkled. 'Please go on.'

'It was a very close thing.' She glanced at the man beside her and he was watching her. His face calm and difficult to read. 'Malachi did a Sir Walter Raleigh for me in case they were born.'

She saw his lips twitch and smiled back. Millicent narrowed her eyes as she thought about that. Turned to her grandson. 'You put your suit jacket on the floor?' Malachi shrugged and his grandmother laughed. 'Terrifying, I'm sure, but it is a little like a soap opera.'

'Except they forced the doors open and we made it to the birthing suite in time.'

'Most fortuitous,' Malachi said.

'Malachi caught Bastian, who was born in the wheelchair, and Bennett was born on the bed less than a minute later.'

'She was amazing,' said Malachi. 'Composed throughout.'

Lisandra pretended to shake her head in mock disapproval. 'And then you disappeared.'

'People were looking after you.' He lifted his chin. 'I was due in Theatre.'

'I'm teasing you.' He was just that little bit more serious than expected sometimes. 'I was in good hands.'

Their eyes met and his were slightly narrowed. 'Yes. You were.'

The cup in his grandmother's hand returned to the saucer with a gentle rattle. 'So, you only just met. No previous acquaintance?'

'None.' Lisandra looked at her. 'But very glad we did meet.' Malachi smiled at her.

'How did you end up here?'

'Gran.' Malachi's voice held disapproval, but Lisandra wanted no misunderstandings.

'When Malachi visited me that same evening, he discovered I had no family. When, a week later, my accommodation fell through, he offered his loft, until the wonderful Ginny could find me a new lease. They both helped me move in last night until Malachi was called back to the hospital.'

Millicent looked thoughtfully approving, which was not what Lisandra had expected. 'Ginny is a magician.' There was no malice or innuendo in her words. 'And Malachi has always been concerned for others. Malachi is rarely here. I can see the sense of the idea.'

A single low wail came from the lounge room and Lisandra put down her cup.

Malachi put out his hand. 'I'll get him. Finish your coffee.'

She sank back into her chair as Malachi strode into the house.

Millicent blinked her wide eyes. 'I suppose he must be good with babies, with his profession,' she said, 'but I've never seen him with one.'

'He's had a bit of practice over the last week,' Lisandra said. 'He came every evening before he went home and was often handed a baby by the midwives when he arrived.'

'Did you think it was odd that he visited when he wasn't your specialist?'

'No. We shared an intense few minutes and trust was established.' She shrugged. 'His were very short visits. I looked forward to both Malachi and Ginny dropping in. They were the only ones apart from the midwives.'

Millicent's brows drew together. 'Where is your family? Your friends?'

'No family. My midwifery friends are in Melbourne. I was invited by the baby's grandparents to visit, when their father first died, so his parents could know their grandchildren. By the time I arrived that welcome had been rescinded. It was a shock. I hadn't expected his father to blame me for something beyond my control, but he did. Richard's mother has little choice, I think. I have savings, but, as we had been living together for less than a year, I'm on my own with the boys.' And it shouldn't still hurt but it did.

Millicent said, 'Grief does odd things to people. I'm sorry that happened to you.'

Malachi had said something very similar. Which made her wonder if something had occurred in their family.

Malachi strolled back into the room with Bastian looking comfortable in the crook of his arm. It was funny how she could tell the boys apart even though they looked so similar. More of an expression than different facial features, which was also odd considering the boys were so young. Bastian yawned in the big man's hold.

Millicent watched her grandson with an amused glint in her eye. 'I despaired that he would ever have a child but maybe there's hope for him yet.'

'Talking about me, not to me, Gran?'

'Of course, darling, you know I like to do that.'

Lisandra hid her smile and finished the dregs in her cup. 'Here. I'll take him.' She reached up and Malachi placed her son in her arms. 'He might sit for a few moments more before the noise escalates.'

As the transfer completed another low complaint came from inside the apartment. Malachi's lips twitched and he turned and went back into the room to retrieve the one left behind.

'I see what you mean about them being

aware of each other and missing out,' Millicent said. 'May I hold this one?'

Lisandra stood up. Juggling the baby as she rose. 'Normally I'd say yes. It's been lovely to meet you, Millicent, but I think I'll take the boys back upstairs to change and settle them.'

'Of course. Thank you for coming down to meet me on such short notice.'

Lisandra smiled and Malachi returned with Bennett. 'I'm going back upstairs while the complaints are low-key. I've decided to put them back in the pram and leave while I'm ahead.'

'Would you like a hand?'

'I'll be fine, thank you. If you could hold the front door when we get there, that would be great.' She slid Bastian into his pram bed and then took Bennett to do the same. Over her shoulder she said, 'I left the main doors open upstairs so I could get in easy when I came back.'

'Excellent idea.' Malachi moved to the door to open the way for her. He slid the chock under the wood and pressed the lift button.

'I think I'll reverse in. It worked well last time.' Lisandra made a wide circle in the roomy foyer. Malachi shook his head in appreciation as she manhandled the long pram. 'You're doing so well.'

Lisandra smiled. 'You sound like a midwife more than the obstetrician.'

He screwed his face. 'Heaven forbid.'

Did Malachi just make a joke? She grinned at him. 'You wish.'

He smiled back at her. 'Sometimes.' The lift arrived and she reversed in. 'Have a good day.'

'You, too. Thanks for the opportunity to meet your grandmother.' She watched him nod as the doors closed. And no doubt that would be the last she saw of Malachi for the weekend.

CHAPTER NINE

Malachi

As the lift doors closed Malachi turned back to his apartment. He nearly bumped into his grandmother standing just inside the front door. She tilted her chin at him as if waiting to pounce. His lips twitched again. Oh, dear. He knew that look.

'Your Lisandra seems a commendable woman.'

'She's not my Lisandra.' Cold reason was the only way to divert her when she was in this mood. 'But yes, I believe her to be admirable,' Malachi said as he closed the door behind his back. 'I'm glad you think so, too.'

'Better than social-climbing Grace, anyway. You do still need a wife.'

Lisandra a wife? He hadn't thought of that. Especially after the disaster of Grace, but the unexpected beauty in that idea rocked him.

And that sort of dreaming, him being a husband and father to the twins, was way out of the realms of possibility. Not a response he wanted to share with his grandmother. Because that could never happen. He would not do to Lisandra what his father had done to his mother. Diversion. Quick. 'I imagine Grace would dispute that label.'

Wherever she tried to lead the discussion he held up his hand and she subsided. He was not going down that path. Certainly not at his grandmother's bidding. 'I believe I'm not looking for a wife, thank you, Gran.'

She waved her manicured fingers at him. 'You like Lisandra.' A statement of fact, apparently, by her tone. 'Why else would you offer her your loft?'

He couldn't explain why. He just knew he wanted to help her. Wanted her safe up there. He lifted his chin. *'Altruism* is a word.'

'Pfft.' Said with a derisive flick of her fingers. *'Oblivious* is also a word and that's what you'd normally be to a woman you met at the hospital.'

His grandmother sat herself comfortably on the lounge and crossed her elegant legs as if settling in for an extended discussion. 'There was something about this particular woman that shook you out of your normal state—no world except work—and made you step out of character.'

She leaned forward and gestured to the seat opposite. 'I want to know what it was.'

With a sigh, he sat as well. He might as well humour her, but he didn't agree with what she was saying. 'Both Ginny and I wanted to help a woman who didn't deserve the unfair misfortunes that had come her way.'

'Mmm-hmm.' He mistrusted that look of mischief in his grandmother's eye. She leaned further forward her gaze fixed on his face as if searching for some hidden mark. 'Do you fancy her?'

Who wouldn't? She was gorgeous. He studied his fingernails. 'The poor woman is a single mother of newborn twins.'

His grandmother sat back as if satisfied. 'And thanks to you there was no disaster at their birth. She has to feel relieved that she met you?'

'I hope so.' He did hope so. Sincerely.

His gran smiled. 'I believe she looks more at ease in your company than Grace.'

They needed to steer away from these discussions. 'Lunch?'

Her brows rose along with her hands. 'At least Lisandra appears even-tempered.'

Lisandra was extremely even-tempered.

Admirably so. Amazing, but he needed to stop comparing her. 'Enough about my new tenant. Where would you like to go for lunch? I hear there's an excellent seafood restaurant just opened in Coolangatta. They're offering lobster mornay. I know that's your favourite.'

Three hours later, once Millicent had driven herself home, Malachi drifted around the apartment and almost wished his phone would ring.

No. Not work. Work wouldn't do it for him today. And since when was that the case? Since his improbable but delightful friendship with the woman upstairs whom he'd known for a week. He was mad.

He couldn't hear any noises from above, but he wondered if Lisandra had the urge to be outside as much as he did.

Perhaps she felt tentative in case there was a problem getting the pram across the road? If so, Malachi's help could solve that problem.

He pulled his phone and texted to her number.

Would you like company to take the boys for a walk? Just in case you need an extra pair of hands. M.

The answer flew back gratifyingly fast.

I'd just been thinking that. Perfect. What time? Now would be good!

She'd probably just fed her babies and tucked them into the pram to sleep. Strolling with happy babies would be so much more relaxing.

Within a minute he'd ascended one floor, knocked and could hear her coming to open the door. His pulse rate rose and he realised he looked forward to seeing her even though it had been just a few hours. His grandmother's words drifted back. *You do still need a wife.* Sadly, and he could admit that much with regret, that scenario was not something he would afflict Lisandra with.

The door opened and she smiled at him as if he was the one person she most hoped to see. Of course. He was the only one with a key, he reminded himself. No big shock.

'Great idea to get out,' she said.

Was it? Pleasure expanded inside him. Excellent. 'Are you ready?'

'Yes.' So, she had needed to get out. Of course, she did. She'd been in hospital for more than seven days. He felt like patting himself on the back.

She went on, 'Apart from the drive here yesterday, it feels like I've been inside for weeks.'

'Not quite.' He smiled at the exaggeration. 'But the day does look pleasant on the paths.'

She glanced at the pram. 'I've been nervous to actually push the stroller into the world on my own for the first excursion.'

'Time for an adventure, then.' He gestured to the wheels. 'Can I try to reverse into the lift?' She made it look easy and he wondered if it really was.

'Sure. I'll grab my hat and cross-body bag.' Which she did while he manoeuvred the long pram and in less than a minute they were in the lift with two babies going down to the ground level. Everything seemed to happen fast when Lisandra was around.

'My grandmother was impressed with the way you handle the boys. Though…' he remembered how Lisandra had arrived at his door with her babies perfectly settled and her face serene '… I'm not surprised she was impressed.' He couldn't remember when he'd last admired a woman so much.

Her eyes widened. 'Why on earth…?'

'You were splendid.'

The dazzling smile she flashed seemed to

flow through him from top to toe. A shock of pleasure.

'Splendid is such an old-fashioned word,' she replied softly. 'But a lovely compliment. Thank you.'

He wasn't finished. 'You were also decisive when you decided to go home. All things my grandmother admires.'

She blinked at him as if she couldn't understand why he would be delighted. Good grief. She had no idea how wonderful she was.

'Thank you, Malachi. For everything.'

'What for?' Now he was the one honestly puzzled.

'Your confusion says a lot for your innate generosity. It would be too easy to abuse your trust. I'm determined not to.'

'I still don't understand.'

She waved her hand encompassing the flats above them and the world outside as the doors opened. 'For the use of your loft in my hour of need. For your friendship and kindness, like coming with me now.'

He lifted one hand from the stroller to brush the comment away. 'I'm selfish. I want people to think I'm clever enough to have twins and a beautiful woman on my arm.' The truth in the statement startled him. Where the heck had that come from? He didn't have time for a woman on his arm. Yet he'd made time for Lisandra. He thought about that. Shied away. Remembered his own childhood when his father was never there.

He did not have the skills to be a father to one baby—let alone twins.

'You're teasing again.' She smiled back at him. 'You're much less serious out of work.'

'I was serious.' But he smiled when he said it. She made him smile. She made the sun shine brighter and he let his misgivings slide away just for today.

They slipped out onto the footpath, which thankfully was deserted on their side of the street as he worked out how to steer the long pram. He aimed for the pedestrian crossing.

She pointed to the pram. 'I need to do this to make sure it's safe for me to be in charge of an expedition.'

He stopped and stepped back at once. 'Of course, sorry, I forgot. Though I do have great faith in your abilities.'

'Thanks for that,' she murmured with a shake of her head. 'Let's see if it's true.'

Once across the busy road—she seemed to find getting on and off the kerb not too bad—Lisandra pushed the pram along the tree-shaded path. He walked beside her. Strange how pleasant it was just walking along with

Lisandra and her boys asleep, the breeze blowing, and the world passing them safely to the side. People on bikes and skateboards and motorised scooters zipped past.

He stood to the right between her and the path traffic, ensuring she wouldn't be bumped.

To her left, waves crashed onto the shore and seagulls squawked and winged in arcs of white against the blue of sky and gold of the sand.

She sighed, her face happy. 'It's beautiful, today.'

He realised she made it beautiful for him. He took a deep breath and let it out. Sea and salt and a tendril of Lisandra's scent like a drug slowing him down to have time to enjoy. 'I'm glad you think so. This is very pleasant. I don't often go out in the afternoons, just early mornings for a run.'

She glanced at him. Apparently liking what she saw because she said, 'I must watch out for you. Nothing nicer than watching a strong, athletic man run past.' She winked and it was his turn to shake his head at her.

She thought he was strong and athletic? 'Now you're teasing me.'

'A little.' Her eyes were full of mischief and his heart gave another of those odd gallops of pleasure.

A huge red kite with trailing board rider zipped by on the waves out from the shore. She laughed as the rider bumped off one wave and skipped onto the next. 'I'd love to try wave-surfing with those kites.'

He'd often thought so but doubted he would ever actually try. 'It looks like it requires some skill.'

'But fun.' She grinned across at him and he smiled back. 'Maybe one day my boys will try it.'

She was so brave. Her boys would be too. 'I don't doubt it.' But not him. He'd be at work. Not doing dad things. Whatever they were. But the future man she should choose for the boys' father, he would know how to teach his boys about life and love. And sail boarding.

For Malachi there was always work.

CHAPTER TEN

Lisandra

LISANDRA WATCHED THE unexpected animation she'd enjoyed so much disappear from Malachi's face. What did she say? Before she could ask, Bastian wailed, and she stopped the pram to lift him from his capsule. 'Do you have wind, my baby?'

Malachi stopped as well. 'Probably. Do you want me to take him or push the pram?'

She gestured to a vacant bench. 'Let's sit there overlooking the water. I can sort his request and enjoy the view. No doubt his brother will ask to be lifted as well.'

Malachi pushed the pram over the bumpy grass to stop beside the bench. Of course, Bennett grizzled and moaned when the motion ceased. 'Is your brother getting all the attention and you are not?' He glanced at Lisandra. 'May I lift him?'

It wasn't necessary but she really liked the way he asked before he reached for the boys. 'Go for it. Thank you.'

Malachi sat beside her, his big arms and solid thighs close to hers, giving off heat though they weren't actually touching—the subtle brush of closeness. He held Bennett in the crook of his arm just as Bastian let out an impressive burp. 'Good grief. Such a big noise for a small gentleman.'

And that was why Malachi charmed her. He projected the busy Gold Coast specialist, the decisive obstetrician and senior consultant but at heart he was such an old-fashioned guy brimming with kindness. Between them, he and Ginny had restored her shattered faith in the human race.

She lay Bastian in the crease between her legs and held out her hands. 'Give him to me and if you could take this one now, we can almost move on. Tuck him back into his capsule if you can without him complaining. I'll see if I can get his brother to do the same. That might give us another half-hour of walking before we need to go back.'

Ten minutes later and between the two of them they resettled the boys in the pram and pushed forward along the wide sweep of path that reached out around the headland towards

Coolangatta. The waves crashed beside them, surfboards and riders skimmed along the bigger waves, and seagulls wheeled.

'This is glorious. It feels so good to get out.' Even she could hear that enormous relief in the words. Not very flattering considering the boon she'd been given with her accommodation.

She turned to look at him. 'Not that I'm not living the dream inside your gorgeous loft.'

Malachi laughed. Not something he did often and the flash of teeth made him even more handsome. 'I understand what you're saying. No offence taken.' His understanding warmed the cold parts left from her loss and Richard's parents' rejection. She really needed to move on from letting others bring down her mood.

'Thank you.'

'I do wish you'd stop saying that.' She felt his gaze on her as she steered the long pram. 'Twins on your own is a very big responsibility. I'm just helping a little where I can. I'm not really putting myself out. But I do wonder if perhaps you could use more consistent help.'

She snorted. As if that were an option. She joked, 'Are you moving in with me?'

He blinked and then laughed again. Such

a fabulous deep, basso laugh. 'Technically…'
He let the sentence trail off.

'What?'

'You moved in with me.'

She shook her head at her own mental slow-
ness. 'I asked for that.'

'You did.' They smiled at each other and
Bastian whimpered. Malachi looked thoughtfully down at the grimacing infant. 'Are we
going back?'

'Best to quit while we're ahead.' She checked
the path for a gap in traffic and swung the
pram in a wide circle until they were heading
the other way. In fact, she was tired as well,
and the pram had morphed to heavy.

'May I push for a while?' And there it was.
His awareness of her. His watchful care and
attention to her needs. Even Richard hadn't
been that observant.

'Thank you. Suddenly, I am flagging a bit.'

He stepped in behind her, put his arms
on her waist and shifted her sideways. His
hands were warm and strong and very gentle. She resisted the urge to lean back into
him but that wasn't their relationship. He
was her friend, not her lover. What a ridiculous thought. The last thing she needed was
a lover. But if she ever had one again… He
would be like Malachi.

'You expect too much of yourself.' He took control of the push bar.

She lifted her chin. 'I'm not a wilting flower.'

He smiled. 'Just a little. Just at this moment.' And the words were all the more sweet because she knew it wasn't his default to tease. Trying hard to be amusing for her. She wanted to hug him. And thank him again but he'd asked her not to. She'd have to figure out some way of showing him just how much his kindness meant to her.

Once back in the loft she pushed the boys' pram into their bedroom and swung the door to leaving only a crack. 'Would you like a coffee? You could show me how to use that machine.'

'Excellent idea.' But when he shifted his wide shoulders and solid chest into the small narrow room she knew it would be difficult. They'd have to squish up together in the tiny butler's pantry to have the coffee lesson. His breadth and long arms and her tucked in beside him would be very, very cosy.

She saw Malachi glance left and right in the small space and raise his brows. 'Not much room. Perhaps I'll just make you a coffee and the next time you come down to my apartment I can show you then. We have the same machine.'

She tried not to sag with relief. 'A fine resolution to the problem.' Now *she* sounded old-fashioned, which made her lips twitch. 'I could get spoiled with all this attention.'

A sharp cry drifted from the boys' room. 'I doubt it,' Malachi said dryly and watched her walk away.

By the time she returned a steaming latte rested beside the chair she favoured and Malachi sat opposite with his own cup. When she eased down they raised their small mugs together in unison and sipped. Perfect. Of course. The man's brew was barista quality.

He said, 'Do you feel you need anything else? Something that would make it easier to manage?'

'I have everything I need. Thank you.'

He waved his hand in complaint.

She lifted her mug. 'I have to be polite.'

Malachi smiled. 'You don't have to be anything. This is your home until you choose to leave.'

She bit back another thank you. 'It will get easier as the boys get older and I establish a routine.'

He sat opposite her. One elegant leg crossed, relaxed, more relaxed than she could remember seeing him, with an odd smile in his eyes. 'How do you see that routine?'

She waved her hand dismissively. 'Seriously?'

'Yes. Seriously.' He was watching her face as if it was a pastime he could really enjoy. Just friends. That was all they were. Nothing more.

She pushed past that ridiculous thought. 'Something like…feed, breakfast, feed, walk with pram, feed, nap.' She stopped and his eyes were twinkling.

'Please go on,' he said. 'This is riveting.'

She laughed. 'Where was I?'

'Nap,' he said, 'and I'm very pleased to hear you do plan one.'

'I plan two. They're very short naps.' She shook her head at him paying enough attention to be able to answer her rhetorical question.

He waved her on. 'Please. Give me the rest.'

'More?'

A decisive nod. 'More.'

She pretended to tick them off her fingers. 'Feed, lunch, feed, nap, online shop, clean, business time, then feed and bathing the boys.' Inclined her head sagely as if imparting a great secret. 'Bathing being a very busy time. Feed, dinner, sleep.'

His mouth curved. 'Sounds like a demand-
ing day.'

'It does.' She shrugged. 'But that's what
routines with breastfed twins are. Luckily, it
comes with smiles and coos, and magic moments too precious to miss.'

His face turned serious. 'I can see that. I'm
going to miss it all while I'm at work.'

'I know. Please don't feel left out. We'll be
thinking of you as we watch the waves.' This
conversation was crazy. Silly. Fun.

'You won't have time.'

She smiled and didn't say anything else.
Just sighed back in her seat, sipped her coffee, and savoured this delightful adult company for the time she had.

'Would you like to go to lunch next Saturday?' His offer surprised her.

She huffed out a small laugh. 'Where can
we take a pram that's nearly two metres long?'

'Good point. Would you like to have lunch
with me next Saturday and we'll order in?
There's a new seafood restaurant that I'm sure
I could persuade to provide takeaway.'

'That does sound much easier. Aren't you
on call next weekend?'

'No. I declined. I haven't had a weekend off
hospital call for six months and I've called in

some favours for the next four weeks. Apart from my own patients, of course.'

He declined? She'd have to ask Ginny how often that happened.

He sipped his coffee with obvious relish. 'And I'm quite enjoying the difference.'

She huffed again. 'I don't see how you can be. You brought your work to your place when you invited the boys and me into your home.'

'You and your small family are not work. Or in my home. And on that note, I don't want to outstay my welcome—so I'll leave you.'

He stood. 'Thank you for your hospitality, Lisandra.' He paused. 'A favour?'

'Of course.'

'When I'm home early—I'll text you if it's before six—could you let me know when the bath-time shenanigans are about to start and maybe I could help?'

'He said that?' Ginny's voice held astonishment. It was Monday night and Ginny had phoned and reminded Lisandra she'd said she would drop in after work Mondays and Wednesdays.

Lisandra was very glad to open the door to her as she hadn't spoken to any adults since Malachi on Saturday.

'I hope you're going to let him help,' Ginny

added. 'Malachi needs to understand he deserves a life of his own, not just to be on call for everybody else.'

Lisandra spread her hands out in disbelief. 'I don't think him helping me bath the boys is a favour to him.'

Ginny bustled in and placed a small, vigorous-looking African violet on the kitchen bench. 'You need flowers in here.' She turned back to Lisandra. 'As far as I'm concerned, you're giving a gift by showing him there's more to life than being at the beck and call of a hospital service.'

That didn't make sense, or not in the context of him coming here to help her with the babies. 'Malachi loves his job. He wants to be there for his patients.'

'Yes, but the hospital takes advantage of him and most of the other doctors do as well. He's the go-to doctor for their social lives and all the patients on the floor. It will run him into the ground if something or someone doesn't make him change.'

'At least he's not doing every weekend on call this month.'

'That's why I brought you the violet. To say thank you.'

Lisandra stepped forward and hugged Ginny. 'You're a doll. I don't deserve it, but

I love it. I love the fact that you worry about Malachi. And in the short time that I've been here we have smiled a lot over the babies. So maybe we're not too much of a burden so far.'

'Have you met Millicent yet?' Ginny whispered.

Lisandra laughed. 'Yes. I met his grandmother. The first morning after I arrived.'

'How was she?'

'Fine.'

'She must have liked you. If she didn't you would have known. She was scathing about Grace.'

CHAPTER ELEVEN

Malachi

To HIS SURPRISE, and not a little machination on Ginny's part, Malachi managed to make the boys' bath time for Tuesday and Wednesday nights for the first week. It could have possibly been a world record for him to leave work in the daylight two days in a row.

At the actual events he had been a tad hamfisted at drying wet babies and easing small feet into trouser legs, but he was getting the hang of it. All he knew was that he enjoyed every second and Lisandra seemed glad of his assistance.

Then all of a sudden it was Saturday again and he was off work and he had a date with Lisandra for takeaway lunch. He'd been looking forward to it all week.

Lisandra had suggested fish and chips, but

he'd requested the pleasure of her company at one p.m. downstairs for a sumptuous banquet, 'so don't eat much for breakfast'.

She'd laughed and agreed to be on time with the pram, and he'd set the table outside on his patio, with crystal and non-alcoholic wine prepared to spoil a woman who deserved a little fuss.

Keen for something special, Malachi was now on his way to collect a seafood smorgasbord from his new favourite restaurant, where, if he hadn't given them a very generous tip, they would still be grumbling about the idea of takeaway.

He'd called it a banquet for a private party and they'd grudgingly accepted the order.

Ten minutes later, soup tureens and foil-covered platters nestled in the front seat and on the floor of his convertible, Malachi carefully drove back to the apartments.

Thank goodness the lifts weren't busy, he thought as he juggled his loads, and hoped the boys would be settled and sanguine while he and Lisandra feasted.

Fifteen minutes later she knocked at the door and just before he opened it, his phone rang.

Torn between answering the door and the

phone he did both, regretting the false start to what was supposed to be a perfect day.

'Come in,' he said. 'Sorry...' He was gesturing to the phone and saying, 'Dr Madden?'

And that was when it all went wrong. He watched as Lisandra smiled and sailed past with the pram, parking the boys in the same spot as last week, and stepping out onto the outdoor area and his laden table.

He watched her turn back with an appreciative smile just as the words sank in. *Urgent. Worrying foetal heart sounds. His very stressed IVF patient.* He knew he had to go.

'I'm on my way,' he said, and sighed for all of them. Lisandra, of course, waved him away.

'Go. We'll do dinner,' she said. And he felt as if a load had shifted off him.

He didn't make dinner, more like late supper, and he ate upstairs in Lisandra's loft. She'd already had hers at his insistence, but it was still special. She'd sorted it all, his table cleared, everything packaged and carefully managed to preserve the food. It had been delicious, but it had brought home all the reasons he could never be a person a woman and her children could rely on.

* * *

Malachi made bath time twice through the next week. Three the next and four the following week. The boys were seven weeks old now.

On that Saturday evening, the thirty-seventh day that Lisandra had lived above his apartment, Malachi arrived with boxes of pizza—an idea he'd thought might make Lisandra smile—which he left in the kitchen nook for reheating.

Her happy hello of welcome made the last couple of hours of fast work worthwhile as they bathed the boys, smiling at the infant antics and working in unison. After that first week beside the mini tub he had it down pat. Lisandra was sure and speedy while he took a while to work out how to keep the young fellows happy as he dried and dressed them. But it was an easy skill to learn when you were used to babies.

In the beginning while Malachi dried Bastian she'd finished the second bath and redressed her wriggling baby. But, she assured him, his help cut her bath times in half while keeping the boys happy.

By now, he'd almost reached her speed.

'It's amazing how much you've improved

my day without the stress of upset babies at night.'

'By the end of the day you must be tired.'

'A bit. But I bet two months ago you wouldn't have thought you'd be undressing babies before dinner on weekday nights.'

No. He hadn't. 'True.' Not even close. Two months ago he'd dreaded going home to Grace complaining how he couldn't leave the hospital before midnight. He'd actually managed four early nights this week to help Lisandra. Funny that. 'There is an unexpected delight in watching babies as they grow past the hospital stage.'

But he doubted that was his motivating factor. The motivation stood beside him deftly soothing infants. Her hair loose, her face flushed and a beam in her eyes every time he looked at her. She was like a happy flower making him smile.

'I guess doctors are like midwives,' Lisandra said. 'The parents usually go home by day two or three and we don't see their babies again until six weeks.'

'Exactly. We miss out on all this.' He waved his hand at the bath and the splashing baby.

She lifted Bastian out and passed her eldest son into the waiting towel and took the newly undressed Bennett and lowered him in the water.

Malachi squeezed the towel around his little charge and opened it to dab the creases under his arms. Bastian took that chance to unerringly aim a powerful pee stream into the centre of Malachi's shirt.

Lisandra laughed. 'Ha. The big smart doctor was too slow to shut the towel.'

'Hey. Don't shoot the help,' he said to the baby. He pretended to glare at Lisandra. 'And you shouldn't laugh.'

'No. I shouldn't. But it's funny.'

He smiled at her and she smiled back and for several long seconds their gazes met and held. Her eyes were magical grotto pools of blue amusement, and he had to fight the urge to lean forward and take her cheek in his hand. He wanted to move his face towards hers and touch her lips with his. His brain was hinting at things she wasn't ready for, and slowly the laughter in her eyes fell away as she watched him.

Stop, his brain chanted. He had no right. Would never be the person she needed. The father her boys needed.

Malachi looked down at Bastian. 'Let's get you dressed.' He glanced her way without meeting her eyes. 'If you want to top up the boys with a feed I'll put the pizzas in the oven to reheat.'

'Can we sit outside on the veranda?' Head down, he listened hard but couldn't hear any strain in her voice. Just him, then, feeling the need and the angst and the want.

He glanced towards the little balcony. 'We could. Why don't you bring the pram and I can meet you down at my place? I'll reheat the pizzas down there.' He gestured to his damp chest. 'I can change shirts and set the table while you feed and settle them in the pram. There's more room on my deck.'

She slipped Bennett into the pram and took Bastian from him. He'd nearly eased all of the baby's long legs into the pyjama bag. 'Sounds good. Here. I'll finish this. You go change shirts.'

CHAPTER TWELVE

Lisandra

LISANDRA WATCHED MALACHI walk away. Unless she was wrong his long stride was more rapid than usual. Yep. She hadn't been mistaken. He had wanted to kiss her and was stepping away fast from that idea.

Obviously, the thought horrified him, though she wasn't sure why. It certainly should have horrified her, but it didn't. The emotion she was feeling was more along the lines of disappointment that he hadn't followed his instincts.

What would it be like to be kissed by a man other than Richard? She'd really had too few boyfriends to have experience with this. And she certainly hadn't expected to even want the intimacy of kissing to be on her agenda only seven weeks after giving birth. Three years more likely.

But this was Malachi. It wasn't as if she hadn't noticed his wide chest, strong abs under his shirt, or watched him run powerfully along the beach paths. The man was a machine. She'd been awake in the early mornings more than a few times, sitting on the balcony, and enjoyed the sight while the boys fed.

What would it be like to be kissed by big, beautiful, kindness-personified, old-fashioned Malachi? Something stirred, deep and warm inside her, and she knew she'd been avoiding these thoughts.

Would his kiss be chaste? Perhaps not after the heat she'd seen in his eyes tonight. Would it be awkward, because sometimes she felt his awkwardness? Or would the connection she felt between them more each time he came to visit her carry them into a deeper, dangerous connection. Dangerous because she was dreaming if she thought there was a future between them.

She knew there was no future. Knew the time would come. The looming sense of loss when she had to move away and out of his life. She could just imagine his grandmother's horror that the little midwife tenant he'd invited into his home had been invited into his bed.

Crikey. Who could think of sex with all the floppy tummy and breastfeeding involved?

She gave a huff of amusement at the possibility of them actually being able to get to bed, without one or the other of the boys disturbing them. But this type of thought was a concern. Yep, she was starting to fantasise about her landlord. It was time to go. To make new plans. She'd had enough pain.

She needed to get Ginny onto finding her new for-ever home. She suspected Ginny, Malachi's secretary first before her friend, she reminded herself, had gone slow on Lisandra moving out.

She looked down at the baby between her hands and saw that he'd been fully dressed on autopilot. 'Sorry, Bennett. I wasn't paying attention to you. Bad Mummy.' And that was another reason she needed to not think silly, girly thoughts about a prince of a man who was only being kind. Full focus needed to be on her sons, her fatherless sons who needed their mother's undivided attention.

She carried Bennett across to the lounge and wedged him behind the pillow while she scooped Bastian from the pram. Then the juggle to position a baby each side at the breast with her boomerang pillow.

Done. She discovered that if she fed them every time they woke, surely more than they needed, the gaps between the feeds were getting longer, her milk supply increased, and the boys rarely cried. She was getting nearly six hours' sleep in a row most nights and with that came relief from the exhaustion of the first weeks. Fingers crossed it continued. After six weeks she was adept at juggling the boys' demands with living on her own—though Malachi's visits kept her sane.

That was all this warmth inside her was. Her appreciation of the sanity he offered. Nothing else.

Twenty minutes later she had the boys resettled in their pram and was pushing it from the lift through Malachi's open door. He was in the kitchen dishing the pizza onto a round, heated server, cut and ready to eat.

He looked up and smiled, though he didn't meet her eyes. 'I'll take it outside, will I?'

'Sounds great.' She parked the boys in their usual spot against the inside window where the breeze didn't blow on them and followed him out into the evening light.

The last of the sun's rays had gone but there was still light enough to see the final kite-riders flit across the ocean. Down below the streetlights were flicking on and the roar of the traffic had begun to die down.

They both sat and picked up a slice of pizza

but before Malachi could take a bite his phone rang. He put the slice down.

Lisandra stood and moved to the rail over-looking the street to give him privacy. She took a bite of the crunchy crust and melted cheese and listened to Malachi say, 'I'll be there in ten minutes.' Poor Malachi.

He put his phone back in his trouser pocket and stepped across to her. 'I hope everything is all right.'

'A foetal heart trace that needs checking.'

She smiled at him. 'I'm glad they feel they can ring you any time. As a midwife myself, grumpy doctors are a difficult part of the job. I'll wrap your pizza in foil and take the boys back upstairs.'

'Or you could stay put and finish yours. It's all set up here. I might even be back.'

'I'll put yours in foil in the fridge.' She looked at the way he'd set the table with juice and glasses, pizza plates and condiments. She didn't want to waste his efforts. 'If you wish. But only because it looks so lovely here. When I've finished mine I'll go back upstairs.'

He nodded. 'Just pull the door closed when you leave if I'm not back before then.'

'Of course,' she said. But it wouldn't be the same.

So, after wrapping Malachi's pizza in foil,

and on impulse adding a quick note, she placed it in the refrigerator so he didn't get food poisoning. Lisandra sat in solitary splendour and munched her way through three slices of pizza. Seriously, her appetite was off the charts since those boys were born. She'd just risen to tidy her plates when there was a knock at the door.

She remembered that Malachi had said nobody had a key to come up in the lift so perhaps it was a service person. Now the dilemma of whether she should open the door.

Bastian, as if sensing her waver, cried, loudly, and the decision was taken from her. Whoever was out there knew she was here now.

She picked up her son first because she wouldn't be able to concentrate with him distressed in the background. When she opened the door Millicent stood there, dressed in floral silk top and pale trousers.

'Hello, Millicent. I was just leaving. Malachi's been called away.' She hadn't seen his grandmother for a couple of weeks as she'd been away on a cruise.

'Don't leave on my account.'

She felt herself swept by an intense scrutiny. Lisandra kept her smile in place. 'Not on your account.'

'May I come in?'

Lisandra realised she was blocking the door and pushed it wider, hoping she hadn't been rude.

She gestured with her hand to the interior of the apartment. 'You have more right than I do.'

Millicent raised pencilled brows. 'I don't believe that for a moment, my dear.'

Ouch, but before Lisandra could deny that, too, Millicent went on. 'It smells like pizza in here.'

'Yes. Malachi's is wrapped in the fridge in foil but I'm sure he'd share. He suggested I stay until I'd finished mine when he was called away.'

'Very sensible.' Millicent strode across the room to the kitchen and examined the boxes on the bench. 'Vegetarian and Margherita.' Over her shoulder she said, 'It would be easy to miss meals with twins. How is it going with the boys?'

'Fine.'

She left the kitchen and moved across to the pram where Bennett lay with his eyes open staring at a light fixture. 'I can't believe how much they've grown and how busy you must be.'

And was this where she could tell his

grandmother that Malachi was helping her bath them some nights through the week? She didn't think so.

She looked away from Millicent's face to Bastian in her arms. 'We're finding our routines, aren't we, little man?'

'And how's your hunt for a house going?'

And if that wasn't a hint, nothing was. 'Ginny and I have a discussion about possibilities tomorrow.' Fingers crossed. That was as bland and non-committal as she could make it but she had decided that tonight anyway. It wasn't really an untruth. She would make it happen. She'd send her a text and suggest they chat about it tomorrow. It was Sunday, so she wouldn't be interrupting her work. Just her family life—how did she end up being such a drain on the people who were helping her? She did need to get out on her own and stop relying on others.

She needed to leave here before she had to outright lie or say anything else that could be misconstrued. 'Well, lovely to see you. If you'll excuse me, I'm just going to take the boys upstairs. Malachi asked me to pull the door shut when I left, so I'll leave that in your capable hands.'

'Certainly. What time did he leave?'

Lisandra turned her wrist to see the time. 'Thirty minutes ago.'

'Then, I'll leave too. He won't be back for hours. I've never heard of him rushing a visit to the hospital...'

Her words trailed off as the door opened and Malachi walked in.

Lisandra couldn't help thinking how handsome he looked with his well-fitting suit jacket smoothed over his shoulders and his aristocratic features. She could see elements of his grandmother in him but there was nothing that wasn't masculine about Malachi.

His dark brows rose at the sight of Millicent. 'Gran. This is a surprise. Unannounced visits are becoming popular.' There was amusement and wry apology in the glance he sent Lisandra. She hadn't thought he would notice it might be uncomfortable for her for his grandmother to find her in his apartment alone. She'd underestimated his awareness. Again.

Millicent's eyes were sharp. 'A good surprise, I hope?'

'Delightful.'

'As was finding Lisandra here.'

He shifted his gaze from Lisandra to his grandmother. 'Would you like some pizza, Gran?'

'You know I don't eat pizza.'

Lisandra eased away from the two of them with Bastian and began to tuck him into the pram. She didn't know whether to keep moving towards the door or put Malachi's pizza in the oven before he got called out again.

'Then how can I help you, Gran?' This was a different Malachi. A cooler one. Not the awkward man who sometimes struggled with personal relationships, but the suave consultant obstetrician she'd glimpsed in the lift before the drama of the boys' births began.

'I was passing by. Thought I'd drop in on my favourite relative.'

'I'm your only relative.'

'I'm hoping you will remedy that, shortly.'

Lisandra winced. All righty then, this wasn't embarrassing, much. 'I think I'll take the boys upstairs.' Her comment eased into the middle of the awkward silence.

'As you wish,' Malachi said. 'I'll see you tomorrow.'

She nodded and escaped as he stepped back to the door and held it open. With her back to the room she might have pressed the lift button three or more times as she tried to hurry it up, feeling the eyes of the other two people boring into the back of her neck. She'd just push the pram in frontward and get away as fast as she could.

Finally, the lift arrived.

CHAPTER THIRTEEN

Malachi

As MALACHI SHUT his apartment door quietly his voice came out coolly determined. 'I won't have you making Lisandra feel uncomfortable, Grandmother.' No. He wouldn't have anyone making Lisandra feel uncomfortable. Not even himself.

Millicent raised her brows. 'I can't remember the last time you called me Grandmother.'

He inclined his head. 'It is rare I feel the need.'

She pulled a face. 'So, I've irritated you enough by finding your lodger in your unit? Waiting for you to come home from a hospital call, which would normally keep you away for hours?'

And there she went again, interfering where she normally wouldn't have before, and he wondered why she felt the need to now. 'I won't explain the set of circumstances, but I would appreciate if you enlightened me as to the nature of your visit.'

His grandmother moved to the lounge, sat down, and crossed her legs. He suppressed a sigh and thought about his dinner. It looked as if she wasn't going home any time soon.

'Do I have to have a reason to come here?'

'I do feel curious,' he said, as he decided he'd better eat in case the phone rang again, 'as to why you felt the need to drop in without allowing me the option of being prepared to welcome you?'

He took himself to the fridge and removed the foil-wrapped pizzas. There was a small note folded on top of the foil and with his back to his grandmother he opened it.

I do hope you didn't have to wait too long for these. They were scrumptious. Thank you. L.

He smiled to himself and slid the folded scrap into his top pocket and the open foil into the oven. He turned on the reheat cycle.

'Very nicely said, Malachi,' his grandmother's voice broke into his thoughts. 'Perhaps it's just as easy to say I'm not welcome here any more since the lodger arrived.'

He turned back to face her. Had he been harsh? 'That's not true and you know it. Besides, you've only just come back from a holiday.' He crossed the room to her and sat opposite. Crossing his own ankles. 'You are one of my favourite people.'

Gran huffed. 'I'm probably your only favourite person apart from the woman upstairs and her two babies.'

He let that go but the thought occurred to him to wonder if his dear grandmother was jealous. Why? Because he finally had someone else he cared about in his life? 'Not true. There're others. I'm fond of Ginny. And Simon is a good friend.' He considered the direction of their conversation. 'Do you have something against Lisandra?'

She blew out a disgruntled breath. 'It all happened so fast. One minute you escorting Grace and the next this Lisandra is upstairs with her babies or down here in your apartment.'

That made him frown. It just wasn't true. 'Today is only the second day she's been here since you were here last time.'

His grandmother looked taken aback. And not a little chagrined, if he wasn't mistaken. 'Oh. Then I may have jumped to conclusions.'

It did make her aspersions look a bit silly.

But this was taking the coward's way out, Malachi, he mocked himself. 'Of course, I've been to her apartment many times. I try to make it for the boys' bath times if I can get home before six.'

He watched her eyes widen with astonishment closely followed by righteous censure. He'd startled her. Not something he did often. He didn't know why he'd felt he needed to say that because he'd known it would put ideas into his gran's head. Maybe he wanted to hear her thoughts on that. Or he was just being contrary. 'I know you have my best interests at heart. But regardless of the time I spend with Lisandra, I do understand there is no future for us.'

She blinked. 'And why would that be?'

He shrugged, kept his face expressionless, he hoped. 'Her babies need a father. I have no skills there. The last thing I need do is inflict someone like my own father onto young boys.'

'Don't. That's not right.' His grandmother stood far too quickly for a lady of her age and swooped in next to him on the sofa. She touched his leg. Her face held distress. He regretted that. He hadn't meant to upset her.

'When the time comes you will be a wonderful father.'

His own turn to grimace. 'Apart from the fact that I'm never home and had no role model to learn from?'

'Well, you managed to get home tonight,' his grandmother said wryly. 'Surely a trip to the hospital and back in half an hour is a world record for you.'

'Perhaps.' He had to give her that. 'But tonight's patient issue was an easy problem to solve.'

'Mmm-hmm,' she said, her tone still dry. 'But normally would you immediately turn around and come home or would you wander off and check everybody else while you were in the vicinity?'

She had him there. 'Perhaps,' he said again.

'Yet you wanted to rush home and share pizza with the woman upstairs.'

'Yes, Gran. I suppose I did.'

His grandmother looked thoughtful and avoided his questioning look. 'She's discussing future housing with your secretary tomorrow. Did you know that?'

First he'd heard. His brow furrowed. 'No. How do you know?'

'Oh…' a suspiciously nonchalant study of fingernails drew his attention '…she mentioned it.'

'Out of the blue? She just mentioned it?' That didn't sound like Lisandra.

Gran pursed her lips. He knew that look. Guilt or guilty about something she'd said. 'I may have asked how her house-hunting was going.'

He compressed the words he wanted to say about interfering grandmothers. She had no right to put stupid ideas into Lisandra's head.

His displeasure must have shown because she patted his leg apologetically. 'I was just trying to make conversation. I didn't know then that you cared for her to this degree.'

'And where did that crazy idea come from?'

'From the emotions on your face when you look at her. Talk about her. Talk about her sons. And she's not immune to you either.' She added with obvious reluctance... 'As long as she's not a gold-digger.'

He stood. Stepped away from her. Looked down and didn't withhold the frown this time. 'I'll pretend you didn't say that.' Fortuitously the alarm rang from the oven as it automatically turned off. 'My pizza is ready. Are you sure you don't want any?'

His grandmother stood, picked up her clutch, and shook her head. 'No, thank you.

I'll take myself home.' She paused. 'I only want you to be happy. You know that?'

He walked over and opened the door for her. 'I know that.'

CHAPTER FOURTEEN

Lisandra

LISANDRA SLID BETWEEN her soft thousand-thread sheets and put her head on the best pillow she'd ever slept on. She'd have to discover where to buy one just like it.

It was early. Not that it was any different from any other night when she went to bed straight after dinner, but tonight, she didn't fall into an instant, dreamless sleep.

She tossed, punched her perfect pillow, turned on the soft sheets and groaned. She was using Malachi. And tomorrow she'd said she'd interrupt Ginny's weekend with her family with her need to search for a new home. She used people. She used to savour her independence, even with Richard. Richard had said he loved that about her.

But surely not wanting to leave just yet was reasonable. The first six weeks after the babies arrived were the most hectic and she didn't want to throw all of their routines into disarray now she looked to be finally gaining some structure to their day.

Not that she could really have structure with twins, but everything was easy here. How long had she really intended to stay here? One day soon she would have to go. Stand on her own two feet.

Here under Malachi's protection there were so many aspects of daily living she didn't have to worry about. Even heavy cleaning. His housekeeper, Mrs Harris, sent her weekly white tornado of cleaning through the loft on a Monday when Lisandra took the boys for their walk along the beachside path.

Groceries delivered, no steps, new appliances that all worked and glorious views to relax with. And Malachi.

Dear Malachi, who underestimated how much he really helped her when nobody else could or would. Helped her just by being one floor away or at the end of a phone call. Who made the tension ease from her shoulders when he walked in with his calmness and presence.

And tonight, with Malachi bathing the boys, he'd been so good with them. So good with her. She had to leave or she'd fall in love with the man, something she wouldn't have believed possible six weeks ago. There was no doubt that misery lay that way.

Would she hurt him when she finally did leave, taking the babies he'd grown accustomed to with her?

His grandmother was right. She'd stayed a long time already and she was using people. Using the kindness of Malachi. She needed to go.

Bennett screamed. A high-pitched squeal that resonated through her like a blade of ice. A scream of fear and anguish that had Lisandra diving from the bed, tangling her feet in the covers in her haste through the open door of her bedroom and into theirs.

She rushed to Bennett's cot and as she passed she glanced into Bastian's small bed. His face shone waxen, white as the sheets, and his body too still. Too still. Oh, God.

She snatched him up and he lolled in her arms like a cloth effigy of himself. She screamed, 'Malachi!' towards the open outside windows, slapped her son's back and breathed a small breath over his mouth and nose then rushed towards the locked door. The door swung inwards and Malachi catapulted through towards her like a dark, shirtless ghost.

She gasped, 'He's not breathing.'

'Table.'

She spun, snatched the soft change mat and threw it down on the table and placed her son gently but swiftly onto his back as Malachi slid in to stand across from her. 'You do the airway. I'll do cardiac massage. Thirty to two.'

She knew that. Her brain started turning again. Thirty compressions to two breaths. He was an infant, not a newborn. Her infant. Her fingers shook as she held her baby's jaw, one hand each side, tilting the tiny face to open his airway. In a nightmare of horror she watched Malachi's strong and so capable fingers press rhythmically down on Bastian's Peter Rabbit pyjamas over his sternum with just the right amount of gentle force.

The fragile cage of ribs sank and rose and Lisandra felt the sobs bubbling at the back of her throat like a swarm of bees. Oh, God.

'Get ready for two breaths,' she heard him say and snapped away from herself to the man in charge. 'Now.'

She breathed two small puffs and watched the tiny chest rise and fall with each breath.

Malachi began the compressions. Again. Counting out loud. 'Get your phone. Ambulance.'

Oh, God. Yes. She spun away and into her room, snatched the phone off the bedside table and sprinted back to Malachi in time to give two more breaths. Punched the three numbers and garbled their address to the despatcher. Two more breaths and this time Bastian gasped. Flexed. Whimpered.

Malachi stopped his compressions. Bastian wailed. Lisandra wailed.

She reached to clutch her baby and cradle him against her breast. Malachi's big, warm arm circled them both and he pulled her into his naked chest. She turned her face into his hot skin and sobbed.

CHAPTER FIFTEEN

Malachi

MALACHI'S ARMS CIRCLED LISANDRA. He was careful not to crush the baby between them. He needed to step back. He needed to watch carefully the colour in Bastian's face. He needed his stethoscope and to make sure the emergency services could get in.

He needed to hold Lisandra.

The tragic wail of another baby, Bennett screaming, made him reluctantly ease his hold and step back.

'I'll get Bennett.' He stroked her face with one finger and lifted his hand to squeeze her shuddering shoulder under the thin straps of summer pyjamas. Her skin was like silk and he stepped away.

'Count his respirations.' She needed something to think about, to remember that they had the skills, that there were two of them who both knew what to do in shocking circumstances like this.

When he stepped into the room tiny fists waved as Bennett struggled in his cot so wildly he seemed almost able to climb out. The baby's eyes swung to his and held.

Malachi felt his heart squeeze. He knew. This baby knew. 'Your brother's okay.' He gathered the fisting child from his portable cot, lifted him until his downy cheek was against his own bare chest and covered that small pyjamaed back with his big hands. 'It's all right, baby. Your brother will be fine.'

He looked over his shoulder back to the lounge room where Lisandra had sunk onto the lounge with Bastian in her arms. Tears streamed down her face in glistening lines, her shoulders taut with tension, and he guessed her legs had almost given under her. Thank God, he had been here for her.

A siren keened in the distance, yes, coming closer. Malachi carried Bennett through to his mother, patting the nappy-covered bottom soothingly with one hand, cradling the back of his downy head with the other.

The baby's cheek felt warm and yet so achingly soft against his bare flesh and he realised he'd never held a newborn skin to skin against him. No wonder babies and parents alike loved it.

Lisandra's phone vibrated where it lay on the table and she looked up at it but didn't rise. Possibly she couldn't. Jelly legs no doubt. Not surprising.

He stopped beside it. 'Could be emergency services.'

'Oh. I should have got it.' Her voice rough with tears and ragged breath.

'I've got it,' he said. 'Okay?'

'Yes. Please.'

'This is Dr Malachi Madden on Lisandra Calhoun's phone. Who is this?'

'Emergency services, Doctor. The ambulance will arrive within two minutes. Is the infant breathing?'

'Yes. Stable at present.'

'Will someone be able to ensure the paramedics can reach the unit?'

'Yes. I'll come down now.' There'd be nobody else to let them in at this time of night. 'I'll leave this phone here with Miss Calhoun but if you need to contact us before I get there use my number.' He rattled off his own. 'I'll disconnect now to go down and meet them.'

He passed a swift assessing glance over Lisandra. The tears had stopped and she wiped them away as her gaze flicked between him and Bennett and back again.

'Will you be all right if I go?' Not that he had much choice, but it was better if she could see that things were meant to be in sequence.

'Of course.' Her voice shook. 'It was so close, Malachi. I nearly lost him.'

'I know. I wish I didn't have to leave you.' Wished he could still be holding her and sharing some of his strength because her eyes looked shattered.

'But someone has to let them in,' she said, and the ragged lift of her mouth dredged up a caricature of a smile. Toughing it out. Making him want to kiss her. God, she was brave.

'I'll grab a shirt on the way through. Be back as fast as I can.'

He tucked Bennett into the lounge beside her with a pillow to hold him. Bennett had stopped crying too, and his eyes were fixed on his brother.

She said softly, 'It was Bennett who saved him. He screamed and that's how I found him.'

Malachi's hand went out by itself and stroked Bennett's cheek with one gentle finger. 'Good boy. Good man.' He forced himself to step back and strode from them fast because the faster he was gone, the quicker he could come back.

He took the stairs two at a time into his own apartment where he grabbed a shirt, his phone and slipped his feet into his beach shoes, glancing once to the open door where he'd been sitting. If he hadn't been outside on the terrace he might not have heard her until it was too late.

Twenty minutes later, Malachi drove as they followed the flashing red lights of the ambulance. He steered Lisandra's car with Bennett strapped in the back in his car seat and Lisandra beside him.

They'd needed baby seats of course and he'd wondered if he should get them in his car, then shaken his head at the idiocy. Out loud he said, 'You'd never fit your baby seats in my convertible.'

He felt her gaze though he didn't turn his head. 'They just don't go with the car,' she said and there was something in her voice that sent a cold chill down his spine. As if she was saying his world and hers were too different.

He could get a different type of car. Stop. Now that was a crazy thought. Did he need to have it spelled out any more clearly that he was in over his head with Lisandra and her sons? And the reason there was no future for him hadn't changed. She needed a man who would be there for her and it was only the merest luck he'd been there tonight. If he was sensible he'd start pulling back. If not tonight, then soon.

As if she'd heard his thoughts, 'I could have driven,' she said, but her voice still shook.

'Could you have?' His voice dry because no way would she have been safe.

She huffed a beat of disgust at herself. 'Not as calmly or smoothly as you're doing, but I would have made it.'

'Bennett asked me to drive.' He tried for a joke, he didn't know why, he'd always been hopeless at them, but she made him want to try. Both of them trying not to think about the last twenty minutes.

The paramedics had asked him if he wanted to go in the back of the vehicle. He'd declined as he believed they could handle anything Bastian offered. Believed in his gut the infant was stable now. His bigger concern had been distraught Lisandra running into the back of a vehicle as she drove and harming herself and Bennett on the way to the hospital.

He'd seen the relief on her face when he'd declined and said, 'I'll bring the mother in.'

The lights of the public hospital drew close

and he parked her car in the doctors' car park as the ambulance went left into the emergency bay. He'd phoned his preferred paediatrician and had no doubt Simon would meet them in Emergency.

'This is the worst night of my life.' Then she shook her head. 'No. When Richard's heart stopped was worse because there was no coming back for him. What if Bastian inherited something from his father's medical history?'

'They'll check all that out,' he said soothingly and thought to himself, she was even braver than he'd realised. 'Were you there when he had his cardiac arrest? Did you attempt to resuscitate him?'

She nodded, her mouth tight, eyes haunted. 'It took that ambulance ten minutes to get there. It felt like hours. I knew by the time they arrived that he wasn't coming back.' Her voice sounded broken but she went on. 'Apparently the clot had been so huge his heart had nothing left to work with.'

Malachi lifted his hand off the steering wheel and touched her fingers. 'That didn't happen to Bastian. He came back fast. Let's go in so Bennett can see his brother's okay. I'll get him and pass him to you.'

He had the feeling she needed to hug her

baby while she walked in. When he climbed out, she stayed staring at the hospital and he understood her fear, felt for her, but they both knew there were efficient and skilled people inside.

By the time he lifted Bennett from his car safety capsule she was out, closing the door, and staring at the large emergency sign.

He walked to her. 'Here. Take Bennett. I'll lock the car.' Not that he needed to do anything except press a button, and as he did lights illuminated her for a moment and he could see the strain in her face.

He lifted her hand in his and her fingers were cold, freezing, shaking. 'You know if I'd had any concerns he'd have a relapse I would have gone with him.'

She shook herself as if frost had skittered along her nerves. 'Yes. Of course. Thank you.' But she hung tight to his hand as they walked towards the big doors.

Inside the lights were bright and he narrowed his eyes as he walked towards the reception desk. 'I'm Dr Madden. This is Sister Calhoun. Her baby has just arrived by the ambulance, Bastian Calhoun. Is Dr Purdy here?'

'Yes, Doctor. He's in Resus Two with Bastian if you'd like to go in.'

Her gaze flicked to Lisandra. 'I'm sorry. If

I could ask a few details, please, before you follow him.' It wasn't really a question and he saw the resigned way Lisandra nodded at the woman. She knew the way hospitals worked.

He said, 'I'll come back and get you in a minute.' Couldn't help notice the relief in her expression.

'Thank you,' she said as she turned reluctantly back to the woman.

Malachi pushed through the swinging plastic doors to the internal corridor and watched the numbers until he came to Resus Two. He knocked and entered.

Simon Purdy looked up from the resuscitation trolley where Bastian squirmed. Typical of Simon's skill with babies, the infant wasn't crying. In fact, Bastian had a fist curled around Simon's stethoscope as he stared into his face. The man was a positive baby whisperer.

To Malachi's relief Bastian's skin colour looked well perfused and they weren't using supplemental oxygen. His pulse oximeter read one hundred per cent and his heart rate ran at a normal speed. Malachi felt the tension ease from his shoulders and knew he needed to get Lisandra in here as quickly as he could to share the relief.

'Ahh. Malachi. I understand this young man

is staying with you?' Clear curiosity shone in Simon's usually serious eyes. Simon was one of the few people Malachi enjoyed the company of on the rare occasions he attended social events. 'Technically. Upstairs, but yes, I've known the twins and their mother since birth.'

'Theirs or yours?' He grinned.

A joke? They were all trying. 'Theirs.'

Simon nodded as if something had been confirmed. 'I thought you had the penthouse?'

'I have. Lisandra and the boys have the loft.'

'And more on that later,' Simon murmured as he looked down at the child. Then he looked up again. 'The woman in the jammed lift?'

Malachi inclined his head. 'Yes.'

Simon looked back at the child. 'He sounds good.' His voice gentle. 'Chest clear. The ambulance report said it took two to three minutes of cardiac massage and respiratory resuscitation to bring him back?'

'Yes.' He thought of Lisandra out there wondering. 'If you hold on a minute I'll retrieve his mother and she can tell you how she found him.'

'Ahh. The dreaded paperwork?'

Malachi nodded in agreement as he left. He could almost feel Lisandra wondering what was going on.

CHAPTER SIXTEEN

Lisandra

WHAT WAS KEEPING MALACHI? Lisandra couldn't
sit. She paced. Even telling herself he'd only
been gone barely two minutes didn't help. The
receptionist had said she'd send a nurse to take
her in but she could barely hold back the need
to ask again. Malachi pushed open the plastic
doors and held them open for her and she blew
out the relief.

'He looks great,' he said, as if that was the
essential greeting. It was. She felt her grip on
Bennett loosen a fraction but she couldn't believe Malachi until she saw Bastian for herself.

'Has the paediatrician said anything?' She
walked beside Malachi as the rush and scurry
of a busy emergency department hurried by
her.

'No. We're waiting for you. Just that the

paramedics mentioned our three minutes of resuscitation. I said you could explain how you found him.'

Beside Malachi it was as if she'd run into a wall. She faltered as if the memory weakened her legs, stupid legs, but Malachi must have noticed because he took her arm.

'He's fine. Bastian will be fine. Would you like me to take Bennett?'

Lisandra's arms tightened. 'No.'

'Through here.' He pushed open a door and then a curtain.

She saw her son under the bright lights of the resuscitator and her eyes flicked to the monitor and the reassuring numbers there, then she glanced at the tall man with the stethoscope around his neck.

'Dr Simon Purdy,' Malachi introduced, 'Lisandra Calhoun.' He added. 'Lisandra's a midwife.'

Dr Purdy stepped forward and took her hand in his big, warm fingers and squeezed. 'It's nice to meet you, but not in frightening circumstances.' He drew her closer to the resuscitation trolley. 'Bastian is well. Doesn't appear to have any sequalae from his event.'

Sequalae—left-over medical problems. Event. Yes, she could call it that.

He went on. 'So far, I can't find anything wrong with him but of course we'll do further tests, which I'll talk about later. Are you able to tell me what alerted you that something was amiss?'

Lisandra dragged in a breath and consciously blew it out again slowly. She dropped her shoulders and forced herself to think back to that horrible moment when this nightmare began. 'I was in bed. Thankfully I couldn't sleep. And then Bennett…' She looked down at the baby in her arms. 'Bennett let out the most blood-curdling scream I've ever heard.' Her gaze drifted to Malachi. 'I never want to hear that sound again, anyway…'

She looked back at Dr Purdy. 'I scrambled out of bed towards Bennett and as I passed Bastian's cot I saw he didn't look right. Too pale. Unnaturally still.' Her breath caught. 'Not breathing.' Her eyes flicked back to the man beside her. 'I just screamed for Malachi.'

Malachi said quietly, 'The sound carried out of the window from above so I wasn't there much later than Lisandra.'

Her throat had closed at the shocking memories and somewhere inside she knew that a part of her reaction was left over from when she'd lost Richard.

She waved him on to take over the tale as she cupped her hands over her nose and mouth and closed her eyes.

Malachi continued the history while she breathed. 'We transferred him to the dining-room table and I began cardiac massage while Lisandra attended to the respiratory resuscitation.'

'How long do you think it was until you had a response, Lisandra?'

Lisandra took her hands away from her face and straightened her shoulders. She knew that Dr Purdy probably had this information from the paramedics and possibly even from Malachi, but wanted her opinion as well. 'It felt like for ever, but five rounds of thirty seconds would make it just over two and a half minutes.' She looked at Malachi and he nodded his head in agreement.

Dr Purdy said, 'The most likely cause is stomach content aspiration, causing a vagal response and arrhythmia, but we may never know why Bastian stopped breathing.'

She squeezed her hands together and imagined not knowing if her baby would stop breathing some other time. 'You mentioned tests?'

'Yes. Blood tests and a scan of his lungs

and a chest X-ray, if you're happy with us doing that?'

'Of course. Do whatever tests you think you'll need.' She looked at Malachi and then back at Dr Purdy. 'The twins' father died of a massive blood clot in the heart nine months ago.'

'I'm sorry for your loss.'

'Thank you. Of course I'm worried about cardiac anomaly being a cause.'

'At this stage I think that scenario is unlikely, but we'll certainly look into it as much as we can without being invasive.'

'Thank you.'

'You're welcome. We'll keep him overnight at least. Are you breastfeeding?'

'Yes. Fully.'

He gave her an admiring nod. 'Breastfeeding twins is no light undertaking. Both boys look well nourished and despite tonight's adventure they appear well. I see no reason why Bastian can't return to normal breastfeeds as soon as he's hungry. We'll arrange a room for you and his twin to stay near him and be available for feeds.'

'Bennett,' Malachi said. 'His brother's name is Bennett.'

Dr Purdy inclined his head and smiled. 'Bastian and Bennett. They're great names.'

* * *

Two hours later Lisandra sat in a room a few doors down from the paediatric intensive care, feeding Bennett, wishing for company. She'd just left Bastian in the ward where he would be strictly cardiac and respiratory monitored throughout the night.

Malachi had left after an hour to answer a call, in her car, to reach the maternity hospital, which was almost amusing, but she had no doubt he'd sort the logistics of vehicle change-overs tomorrow. Or Ginny would. And there she was using people again, but she couldn't imagine how she would have coped if she'd been on her own.

She rubbed her temples and held back a sob. This whole thing was a nightmare.

Bennett pulled away from her breast and tilted his head towards her, his brows coming together in a frown. He gurgled and cooed and she blew out a whoosh of breath and smiled at him. 'You're my little hero, you know that, don't you?'

Bennett cooed again.

Tension in her neck eased slightly as she lifted him up over her shoulder to rub his back. 'Yes, baby. Mummy needs to have a sleep soon and put an end to this horrible day.'

She looked up at the sound of a brief knock.

She knew that knock. Malachi was back and suddenly her world straightened.

The door opened and his head ducked around as if he was unsure if she was sleeping.

'I'm awake. Come in. Please.'

The rest of him appeared. Dear, dear Malachi. She shouldn't be so very glad to see him. He carried a disposable cup in his hand and the aroma of hot chocolate drifted across the room.

'I thought you might prefer this to a sleeping tablet.' His smile warmed her. There he went again doing something unobtrusively kind and wonderful for her.

'That is exactly what I would love. Thank you.'

'Can I take Bennett for you while you sip?'

In answer she lifted the baby towards him. 'I was just burping him. He's almost ready for his bed.'

'You look ready for your bed.' His concerned gaze travelled over her face.

She looked down at herself and grimaced. 'At least I'm in my pyjamas. And glad you suggested I bring a small bag.' She'd packed one while the paramedics and Malachi were ensuring Bastian was stable. 'It means I have my phone charger and something comfortable to sleep in that doesn't belong to the hospital.'

He was still watching her face with concern on his. 'Do you need anything else for the night?'

'No. I'm fine. Thank you for everything, Malachi.' Suddenly her throat stung with the prickles of tears stinging the backs of her eyes as well. She blinked them away. 'I don't know what I would have done without you.'

He came and sat on the bed beside her chair and took her hand in his free one while the other absently patted Bennett's back. 'You don't have to do without me.'

Not now. Or the next few weeks, anyway. Not until she did.

Lisandra turned her face away but he let go of her hand to touch her face and turn it with one finger. 'I don't know what my grandmother said to you today, but there's no rush for you to go anywhere, any time. I enjoy having you all upstairs.'

It was as if he'd seen through to what was most worrying for her. She searched his face. 'How will I know when I've outstayed my welcome?'

He smiled and shook his head. 'You could never outstay your welcome. The place would echo with emptiness if you all left.' He stood up. 'But that's for another day.'

He leant forward and brushed her cheek with his lips. His warm mouth smoothing her face as if in blessing. 'You did well today. Try to get some sleep between the feeds. I'll see if I can get here for Simon's ward round to-morrow morning.'

She knew he did a ward round on Sundays for his own patients at the maternity hospital. 'You don't need to.'

His face turned stern. 'I'll be here. Unless you don't want me to be?'

Of course she wanted him. 'Thank you. I would like that.' Time to be honest if he thought she didn't want him. She didn't want him to leave now, let alone not come back.

CHAPTER SEVENTEEN

Malachi

THE NEXT MORNING, he'd barely slept for worrying, Malachi found Lisandra in the paediatric intensive care, her back to the door, her attention focussed on her boys. As he stood at the sink to wash his hands he turned his head to study her for a moment, chin lowered and her lovely neck exposed as her hair fell away to the sides as she bent over Bastion.

Bennett lay in the pram beside her.

He knew now she'd become more than a friend since she'd moved in and he thought back to his grandmother's words.

He had grown very fond of Lisandra but fond wasn't the feeling that had made him toss restlessly in his bed last night. It was more than that. Way more. And complicated. He'd been gutted at the thought of anything happening to Bastian or Bennett and his heart had ached at the distress it all caused Lisandra. He cared. For all of them. Deeply.

He wanted to make her move down to his apartment and tell her she had to stay for ever. But that was ridiculous.

He was under no illusions about his worth in the husband and father stakes. Lisandra deserved a husband who would be there for her—not one like him, who would be absent or called away at any moment. The boys deserved a father who knew how to do all the things a young boy needed to do. One who would turn up for the important stuff. Unlike him.

He should step back. Because, if he wasn't careful, when she did leave and find a deserving partner this would become one of the most painful goodbyes of his life.

As if she sensed him, she looked up and smiled, and instead of stepping back he stepped towards her, crossing the distance between them in moments. 'Good morning, Lisandra. How did you sleep?'

'Surprisingly well between feeds. No further problems with Bastian overnight.'

His chest eased with her release of worry—though his own concern had been decreased by Simon's early phone call. 'Excellent.'

Her turn to study him. 'And you? Were you called out after you left here? You look tired.'

He heard a familiar deep rumble from behind him and Simon saved him from answering. He turned to see the paediatrician walking with the ward intensivist towards them. Malachi eased himself back to ensure Lisandra had front and centre but his mind whirled with wonder. She'd noticed he looked tired?

When Bennett started to fidget and complain at lack of attention, without thought, Malachi reached into the pram and lifted the boy to his chest, pulling his little body into him. 'Shh… Your mother is talking. She needs to discuss today's plans with Simon.'

Simon's brows went up as he blinked. 'You're very handy to have around twins, Malachi. Good to know.'

Malachi lifted his head in pretended surprise. 'Why? Are you planning to have some?' The last thing he needed was Simon to find his fascination with Lisandra and her sons funny. Wasn't going to encourage that.

Simon laughed. 'You and I don't have time for families. Just time to ensure others stay healthy.' Two months ago Malachi would have agreed with him—he wasn't so sure now as he glanced down at the small face and blue eyes peering up at him. He felt a hollow pit of emptiness at the thought of Lisandra and the boys leaving.

Simon turned to Lisandra. 'I hear Bastian behaved well overnight for the nurses. Did you think he fed well?'

She looked tired too, Malachi thought as she answered. 'He seems just the same. No problems with feeds. More hungry, if anything.'

'Good. We'll set up all the tests this morning, even though it's Sunday. Hopefully we'll have them done before lunch and if everything's fine you can take him home this afternoon.'

'Will the tests be done in this hospital?'

'Yes.' Simon stepped in closer to lean over the baby in her arms and lifted his stethoscope to place it on Bastian's chest over his heart.

Nobody spoke as he listened and then stood back. 'Heart sounds perfect. No signs of chest infection but we'll see what the chest X-ray shows. He's had all his surface swabs attended and a throat and nasal swab. The monitoring of his respirations hasn't recorded any apnoea. No alarms or any abnormalities noted during the observations overnight.'

Simon's gaze travelled between Malachi and Lisandra. 'At this stage—' he looked down at Bastian '—I'd say heart arrhythmia caused by milk aspiration. It could have been only a regurgitation during a deep sleep cycle, which in an unusual event caused his heart to miss a beat at the wrong time, but we'll see what the tests show us. I'll be back after lunch to let you know the results. If everything is fine you'll be able to take him home after that.'

Malachi nodded. All as expected. He looked to Lisandra to see if she was satisfied and found her brows lifted at him, asking for his thoughts on the plan. So he said, 'I agree.'

She nodded as if she just needed that and smiled up at Simon. 'I understand. Thank you. I'm happy with that, too.'

'Good.' Simon smiled at them both then fixed his eyes firmly on his friend. 'We'll have to meet up for another dinner, Malachi. I want to hear your news.'

'What news?' He had nothing to share with a winking Simon this morning.

'Just to hear where you're at. Talk soon.' His friend smiled and saluted Lisandra.

'He seems a lovely man,' Lisandra said as she watched Simon walk away.

Hmm. Normally. Being a nosy blighter this morning, Malachi thought, but he said, 'Great paediatrician. We went through med school together. He's the one we want to look at Bastian or Bennett for any problems.'

He needed to get back to a woman he was worried about in labour. He tucked a sleeping Bennett back into the cot. The baby didn't complain. He was getting good at this.

He pulled her car keys from his trouser pocket. 'I moved your vehicle down into the hospital parking last night and caught a cab home, so I have my car, too.' He glanced at his watch. 'Let Ginny know if you need anything. I'm sure she'll phone as soon as she finds out you're here.'

He smiled. Ginny would make sure Lisandra was fine today. 'There are two unexpected caesareans this morning so I might not get back until after lunch. Hopefully before Simon arrives, but if I don't, he'll keep me up to date. Text me if you need me and I'll answer as soon as I can.'

For the first time ever he wished he didn't have a patient waiting for him in Theatre. He wished he could go with Lisandra and Bastian and just be there with them today. Make sure they were fine. And how would Bennett be cared for? He hadn't thought of that. He'd check with Ginny and see what she could do.

CHAPTER EIGHTEEN

Lisandra

LISANDRA WATCHED MALACHI walk away and didn't like the way she felt suddenly alone and vulnerable. That was ridiculous. She had the boys and the boys had her. Her arms tightened on Bastian but after a few words of stern talking to herself she forced them to loosen.

She stood and settled Bastion back into the hospital cot and tucked him in. One of the nurses came and turned the alarm back on— it had kept going off every time she moved him so it had been silenced.

'I'll go back to my room and shower. My breakfast is waiting.' She should pack and be ready to leave, too. Though she had to keep the room until it was positive Bastian was being discharged. 'I'll be back after that.'

The nurse nodded and smiled. 'We'll phone

you if he wakes before then.' She shook her head in admiration. 'It must be so busy.'

'I'm glad they're not triplets.' Lisandra smiled. 'We do have our moments of unusual interest.' A sharp pang squeezed her chest. Like last night. Like finding him lifeless. Like almost losing her son.

The cold washed over her arms at the memories and nausea returned. Last night before Malachi came.

'Dr Madden's very good with them,' the nurse said.

Her sudden panic subsided. She lifted her chin, not seeing the woman in front of her. Seeing Malachi like a rock beside her. 'He is. I'm always very glad of his help.' She looked at the now sleeping Bastian. Turned the pram to leave. 'See you soon.' What would she do without Malachi when the time came to leave?

By the time Lisandra returned to the paediatric ward, Ginny stood beside Bastian's cot with a deep groove creasing her forehead. Her new friend wrung her hands and kept shooting glances at the monitor.

Lisandra came up beside her and touched her shoulder. 'Ginny. What are you doing here?'

Ginny spun and hugged her, warm arms

clasping her middle and for a moment Lisandra closed her eyes and took the hug gratefully. 'Malachi phoned me. Poor baby. Poor you.'

'We're all okay now. We should know more this afternoon. Did Malachi ask you to come?' Of course he did.

It had been so long since someone had comforted her like this.

Not true, her pedantic brain said, Malachi hugged her last night against his bare chest, but she didn't want to think about that with people all around her. That was something for the quiet of her own room when she had time and brain space to sort through those emotions.

Ginny was saying as she squeezed, 'This must have been such a shock.'

'Malachi shouldn't have asked you to come on your Sunday off.'

'Of course he should. He asked if I minded coming to help you with Bennett. I was here like a shot.' She held out her hands as if the choices were a no-brainer. 'I love babysitting and you have to take Bastion for testing.'

Yes, she did, and this would make it so much easier but she felt bad. 'He didn't say anything to me about doing that.'

Ginny waved her hand. 'And that's Malachi. Trying to avoid someone saying thank you.'

Ginny stepped back and looked into Lisandra's face with sudden unease in her eyes. 'I hope you don't mind we've micromanaged you into having a babysitter.'

Lisandra had to laugh. 'I can't think of a sitter I'd rather have for Bennett than you.' And her mushy brain said, *Oh, Malachi, thank you.* 'But he shouldn't have asked.'

Then she remembered her own intentions to intrude on Ginny's weekend to help her find new accommodation—so now who was the pot calling the kettle black?

Still, moving house had been pushed away with the horrific drama of Bastian's health and the tests to come. Despite Simon's reassurance, she needed to be told Bastian's heart was fine. His father's heart hadn't been. Dark dread sat like a black brick at the back of her chest, but she tried not to think of it. The tests would show up anything surely and Ginny would sit with her as they went through the traumatic morning to come.

By eleven a.m. Bastian had roared when he'd had his blood taken, complained his way past

his first ever chest X-ray to see if his lungs
were clear or his heart enlarged.

Had breastfed during the set-up for his
ECG, stopped feeding for the recording, and
gone back to his feed as if bored with all the
wires. As far as Lisandra could tell the test
proved the rhythm of his heart was perfectly
normal from all directions.

Then he'd slept through the ultrasound of
his heart to ensure the chambers and valves
were functioning correctly.

During all the examinations the technicians
had smiled and nodded when Lisandra had
asked if everything was okay…but she needed
to hear it from Simon Purdy and she had to
wait until after lunch for that.

Finally, all the tests were done.

Ginny returned with a freshly made coffee
when all the tests were over and for Lisandra
it made her think of Malachi. Was he worried,
too? Had he heard results she hadn't? Would
he get a chance to come when Simon arrived
with results, between his workload?

But she'd just have to wait and see. And
be grateful for the bonus friend Ginny was.
'You're a star. I'll be fine now, Ginny. You
go. They're both asleep. Thank you so much
for your support.'

'I'm happy to stay.'

Lisandra knew her friend had had two phone calls from home asking about her ETA already.

'It's Sunday. You've worked all week. Go home to your family. Relax. I'll phone you after I see Simon for the official results.'

'If you're sure?'

'I'm sure.' She patted the pram. 'Bennett and I will just doze in the room until Dr Purdy comes,' she reassured her. 'Or Bastian wakes—whichever comes first.'

So, Ginny left, and Lisandra pushed the stroller back to her room to wait. And wait. Lunch came. She ate and waited some more. The phone rang. Bastian had woken.

On her way back to the paediatric wing Lisandra passed a woman sitting outside the glass door seemingly immersed in a book. 'Millicent?'

Millicent looked up and then stood, twisting her hands. 'Oh, Lisandra.' She chewed her lip, which seemed so out of character for the composed woman Lisandra had met before. 'I phoned Malachi this morning and he told me what happened to your dear little baby. I'm so sorry, my dear. What a dreadful worry for you.'

Millicent was the last person she'd expected to run into but her distress was obviously genuine. 'Thank you. It's kind of you to come out to see us here.'

Millicent waved that away. 'What did they say?'

'They ran tests this morning and so far everything appears to have come back normal. I'm waiting for Dr Purdy to give us the all-clear so I can take him home.'

Home. To Malachi's. And wasn't that a clanger of a word when this woman expected her to move out of her grandson's penthouse?

As if she heard her, Millicent hurried on quietly. 'I need to apologise for yesterday.'

Lisandra furrowed her brows. 'Apologise? For what?'

Millicent sighed. 'Sticking my nose in where it wasn't wanted or needed. Or so my grandson said.' She waved her hand before Lisandra could deny. 'I see the changes in Malachi since you've known him and they're all good.'

Lisandra blinked. 'In what way?'

'He's more relaxed with you than I've ever seen him with a woman.' She lifted both hands this time as if in wonder. 'It's a long story and I will share it with you one day.' She shook her head. 'But with the babies?' She blew out a happy breath. 'It's an absolute joy to see him with your boys. I need to thank you for that.'

'I'm not the one who needs thanks. Malachi has been marvellous with us.'

Millicent shook her head. There was a glint of wetness in her eyes and Lisandra felt unexpected tears herself. Though surely her own emotions were due to the horrific last twenty-four hours.

'He had a terrible childhood,' she whispered. 'Brought up by a cold man who belittled him and left him with uncaring staff. I despaired my grandson would ever find happiness.'

Where was this going? Not where it should be heading. 'Malachi's happiness isn't dependent on me. We're just friends, Millicent.'

'I know. He said.' She held up a placating hand. 'It's a start he needed. I hope you stay friends a long, long time with him. And I'm sorry if I was interfering. I'll go now.'

Lisandra felt confused and uncertain about the whole conversation, but she was sure that Millicent was upset. Strange and uncomfortable it might be, but she could see Millicent had come with the best of intentions. 'Don't go. Come in and see Bastian, at least.'

She saw the flare of pleasure. Then she

frowned. 'If Malachi finds me here, I'll be in trouble again.'

Lisandra laughed. 'Malachi adores you, even I can see that, and I doubt you're afraid of anyone, let alone your own grandson.'

'Maybe not.' Millicent lifted her chin. 'And if you're sure you don't mind, I would like to see the little one just for a moment.'

So, they trooped in, washed their hands and made their way to Bastian, who had fallen asleep again oblivious to everybody's worry.

Millicent stared down with a softness in her eyes that surprised and, if she was honest with herself, pleased Lisandra. 'He does look well,' Millicent said quietly. 'I just needed to see him for myself.'

She didn't stay long but there was no doubting her frank relief to see that Bastion looked healthy. Also unexpectedly, she hugged Lisandra before she left. 'I think you're a wonderful mother. This must have been so hard for you. I can't imagine how terrifying it would have been.'

'Thank you, Millicent. Malachi was wonderful.'

The older woman's eyes met hers. 'I'm glad.' She pressed a folded piece of paper into her hand, leaned forward and kissed Lisandra's cheek and then she strode away.

Lisandra unwrapped the piece of paper and saw Millicent's name and mobile phone number with the words *'Ring me any time'* written below in beautiful cursive script. 'Well. That was unexpected,' Lisandra murmured as she watched the door close behind Malachi's grandmother.

'Tell me about it,' said a voice behind her and Lisandra spun to find Simon Purdy standing next to her, his head swivelled to the door. 'From what I believe, Millicent does not grant her hugs often.'

'Really?'

'Really.'

'How well do you know Malachi and his family, Dr Purdy?'

'Simon. I know them well enough for you to call me Simon.' He smiled down at her. 'Malachi and I went to med school together.'

'Yes, he told me that.'

Simon shrugged. 'We worked the same ER in our early days. Malachi was a good friend when I lost my wife. I hoped one day he'd find a good woman, with luck a wonderful one like mine.' He looked down at her. 'Finally, I have hope.'

Her brows drew together. 'Cryptic,' she murmured.

Simon smiled. 'I hear he took himself off call four weekends in a row.'

She still didn't get it. 'And random.' She quirked a brow at him but couldn't help the smile at his mischievous eyes. He was teasing her, but she couldn't pin it down. But her mind was on other things and most of them about what he had to tell her about Bastian.

He raised a brow. 'You want random? You might have to do the running, but I'm cheering for you.' He glanced up, his eyes sparkling. 'Ah, yes. Here he comes.'

CHAPTER NINETEEN

Malachi

MALACHI HAD BEEN busy with two tricky caesarean sections, plus a forceps delivery in
Birthing Unit, all before lunch.

Between each event, he'd hoped to slip back
and see how Lisandra was faring, or at least
send a text, but every time he'd tried, someone had called him away. Maybe it was time
for him to look at taking on a registrar or at
least a resident to lighten his workload.

Simon and Ginny had both suggested it.
He'd always said no. He was beginning to
wonder why.

Still, he was here now, and apparently
his timing proved impeccable as he could
see Simon through the door standing beside
Lisandra.

The two of them smiled at each other, in a
very friendly way, which was a good thing.

Wasn't it? He narrowed his eyes. Simon wasn't a man Lisandra needed—he would be as unreliably available as Malachi with his paediatric workload.

He heard Simon's voice as he pushed through the door. 'Here he comes.'

He crossed the room to Lisandra's side. She looked tired, no surprise there, and he tore his eyes away to peer down at Bastian's hospital cot. The boy looked fine.

Malachi breathed out a sigh of relief, though Lisandra would have contacted him if she'd been worried. Funny how sure he was of that.

Bennett, the little champion, lay in the pram, eyes closed with his fist in his mouth, fast asleep. Malachi lifted his brows at Simon, 'Results back?'

'Not the formal, they'll come tomorrow through the usual channels. I've cc'd you in, Malachi.'

'Excellent.' He nodded. He'd be wanting to read those detailed reports and no doubt Lisandra would too. Easier to have their own copy.

'I was just about to say to Lisandra, I've looked at everything and cardiac structure and function look perfect. Nothing seen that indicates any anomaly or concern. I go back to my original diagnosis of aspiration causing a

cardiac arrhythmia and a prolonged apnoea. I
don't believe there will be detrimental sequalae to this event. And I don't believe Bastian,
or Bennett for that matter, have an increased
risk of something like this happening again.'

They could only pray, Malachi thought.

'Just bad luck?' Lisandra asked.

He nodded. 'Afraid so. And good luck you
both were so good at resuscitation. I'd be
happy for Bastian to go home when you're
ready.'

His friend unobtrusively winked, which
made Malachi frown. 'Something in your
eye, Simon?'

The man grinned but at Malachi's comment
he pulled his face back under control. Simon
was starting to irritate him with his odd be-
haviour, Malachi thought grimly. Thank
goodness Lisandra seemed to have missed all
that silliness as she looked down at Bastian.

Simon hmphed and continued. 'I think it's
important for the next forty-eight hours that
Lisandra has back-up at home. Just someone
she could call out to if she was worried.'

Malachi thought about that. 'Mrs Harris
will be there until five on Monday. I can get
her to come on Tuesday as well and I'll make
sure I get home before she leaves.'

He met Lisandra's eyes. 'If you keep the loft door open, does that work for you?'

'Of course. But what if Mrs Harris doesn't want to work Tuesday?'

He shrugged. Simple. 'Then Ginny or I will have a sickie.'

Simon made a sound that he turned into a cough and Malachi felt strangely tempted to assist him with a forceful blow to the back. Unsympathetically he said, 'You okay?'

'Yes. Sorry. Just inhaled something— maybe at the thought of Dr Madden taking a sickie.' He actually laughed but turned it into another cough. Then held up his hands and continued quickly. 'That sounds like a perfect arrangement.'

He offered his business card to Lisandra. 'If you feel the need for a paediatric consult for the boys at any time you can contact me on my mobile. I'll arrange it with my secretary.'

She took the card. 'Thank you, Simon.'

Malachi held out his hand. 'We appreciate you coming, Simon. Sunday and all.' The men shook hands and Simon clapped Malachi on the back. He wasn't the one coughing, Malachi thought dryly as he winced at the blow.

'Any time.' Simon stepped back. Still grinning. Waved and disappeared.

'He's very good.'

'He is.' Malachi frowned. 'Not usually that jolly, though. Or not for a long time.' He shrugged. 'I've finished at the hospital so I'll follow you home.' He had a burning need to see Lisandra and the boys settled back into the loft again. Last night the apartment had seemed so empty.

Thirty minutes later Lisandra sat, shoes off, on his white leather couch in his apartment, feeding Bennett and Bastian while Malachi brewed a pot of French Earl Grey and set a tray with cups and saucers.

'Would you like a biscuit?' he called across from the kitchen nook and he watched the back of her head shake in denial.

'No, thanks. I still feel a bit sick from the shock of it all.'

He thought so. 'Which is why I asked you to come here first. Just relax, debrief, because I know how hard it is to run things over and over in your mind without actually talking about them to somebody else.'

She turned her head. 'Does that happen often to you? Rehashing without talking to others?'

'Not often,' he said. Only when something doesn't turn out like we all expect, he thought. 'If a baby doesn't breathe. As you know, obstetrics can be the most joyful and the most tragic of professions. The loss of a baby, that promise of the future child being stolen, is always difficult.'

'Yes,' she said softly and he knew she understood.

'It's difficult because we search for things we could have done differently that might or might not have changed the outcome.'

He put the tray on the table between them as she shifted Bennett to her shoulder. 'Here. I'll take him and you'll have a free hand.'

'Thanks.' She repositioned Bastian up to burp him. 'And I certainly understand what you're saying—all that heartbreaking questioning, Malachi. Though it only happened twice in my time in Birthing Unit and both times it proved the baby had no chance of living outside the uterus. Nothing we did would have changed the outcome.'

'Maybe so. But that doesn't help anyone.'

She shook her head in agreement as he watched her. Of course she would understand. She would understand a lot about his work because it ran parallel to hers. 'I like that you get it,' he said. He'd never had a woman friend, except other colleagues of course, who understood the sad as well as the positive aspects of his profession.

'And I like that you get it,' she copied him and they smiled at each other.

Bennett let out a huge burp and Malachi smiled. 'I'm getting better at that.' He looked down at the infant as he carried him to the pram to tuck him in. 'Or maybe Bennett's getting better at that.'

'Probably both,' she said as Bastian also relieved himself of wind.

Malachi stepped forward. 'Stay there. I'll tuck him in too.' He reached over and took him from her hands. Realised this was the first time he'd held him since cardiac massage and his chest tightened in a visceral pull of pain. God, that had been close. He felt his fingers tighten in an emotional response. He couldn't imagine a different scenario where Bastian was lost.

'Have you thought about being a mother-craft nurse?' she teased him and he pulled back from that ghastly memory. Swallowed the horror and moistened his dry mouth. It took a few seconds before he could answer calmly.

'No. But I thought about asking if I could offer you the services of one to give you a break every now and then.' He was serious about getting in help, but she laughed.

'No, thanks. I signed up for this gig and I

have easy babies. Save the mothercraft nurses for the people who have a tough time.'

He finished tucking Bastian in, gave him an extra pat because he could, and thought about her words. She was doing it tough but he didn't argue, just checked that Bennett still looked settled, and then sat opposite her.

He reached for the tea—she'd poured his—and broached the subject that was on both their minds. 'Yesterday was difficult and terrifying but we've done everything we can and can only pray it won't happen again.'

She lifted her teacup, but her hand shook and she put it down again. 'I wondered if I should get a baby apnoea alarm. A breathing pad to lay him on. Something else to keep him safe.' He understood why she'd want one and of course she could if she wanted to, but he wished she wouldn't.

'Of course, that's understandable, maybe for a week or two it could be reassuring,' he said, and they were both silent for a pause. 'But long term they can cause more stress than they alleviate.'

She said quietly, 'That's what we told the mothers, too.'

'The research on apnoea monitors says no evidence was found that they impact the prevention of SIDS in healthy babies.'

'I read that too,' she said. 'But is Bastian normal or at risk?'

They both thought about that.

'Simon said he felt neither of your boys had an increased risk of this happening again.'

'I know.'

'Plus the normal breathing pauses a baby does have make the alarm goes off, and cause more stress.' He watched her, wishing he could help. 'It's hard.'

'He could have died, Malachi.'

'Yes.' And that was just about enough of him sitting opposite her while she was in pain. He stood and moved past the table between them to sit beside her. Slipped his arm around her rigid shoulders and drew her head down onto his shoulder. She sucked in a breath and there was a sob at the end.

He whispered, 'I wish I could take away your worry.'

'I know. You've done a lot. So much.'

He touched her hair. 'I believe the boys will both be fine.'

She nodded against him and he found his lips brushing the silken strands under his mouth. She smelled like herbal shampoo and baby lotion and Lisandra. The most beautiful perfume in the world to him. Quietly he added, 'I like the idea of the loft door open between the two apartments. Until you feel you want to shut it again.'

'And what if I don't want to shut it?'

His heart rate jumped. But he kept his voice low. 'I'd be a happy man.'

CHAPTER TWENTY

Lisandra

LISANDRA HAD SPOKEN the truth, though she probably shouldn't have said it out loud, but her brain was truly fried by the stress of the last twenty-four hours. And she wanted access to Malachi for reassurance.

The wonderful weight of Malachi's arm around her shoulders kept her grounded even when her brain wanted to lose the plot and let her sob. Bastian was safe, she wasn't alone, the boys were happily asleep, and Malachi had her in his arms.

Slowly the tension eased as she breathed in the scent of him, that subtle, spicy aftershave she identified as his, the slab of solid muscle of his chest under her cheek. His warmth. His caring.

His mouth on her hair as he kissed her in sympathy.

What? She froze. There it was again. A gentle caress.

It was only sympathy. Empathy maybe. But she'd take the comfort while she had it.

Besides. It felt wonderful. Against her he felt wonderful. He was wonderful.

It was true. She wanted to keep the door open. Hell. She wanted to sleep down here and if he offered his bed she'd curl up next to him with the boys in the room with them.

'Would you like to sleep down here tonight?' His unexpected words penetrated and made her blink.

'Did you just read my mind?'

He shrugged. 'Maybe you read mine. I was thinking I would lie awake tonight wondering if you were awake worrying.'

'Except neither of us would get to sleep. If we did sleep the boys would wake us up for feeds.'

'True.' She heard the smile in his voice. 'But that would be your job and you would respond.'

Before she could say something, like *gee, thanks*, he went on. 'And when my phone rings and I get called out to the hospital that would be my job and you can snuggle in.'

She laughed. 'You are a beautiful man, Malachi Madden, and I'm so pleased I met you in a lift.' That was the wonderful thing about Malachi—she could say what she thought and he would tell her what he thought right back.

He said, 'Is it time for that lunch, feed, nap part of the day?'

'You remembered that "a day in the life of Lisandra and sons" routine?'

'Every word.'

She believed him. Crazy man. 'It could be time for a nap.'

'I was thinking we could lie, a little like this, on my bed, and maybe close our eyes until the next instalment of that regime appears. Neither of us slept well last night.'

She turned her head. Which was harder than it should have been because her whole body was growing heavy with exhaustion and, because Malachi was right here next to her, she could finally allow the fatigue to overwhelm her. 'You didn't sleep?'

His other hand squeezed her shoulder. 'I worried. About you. About Bastian. Even about Bennett being upset.'

Something precious and fragile inside her opened with slowly spreading petals, unfurling, stretching, reaching for the sunlight that she was beginning to see was the man beside her.

She nodded her heavy head. 'Let's lie down

and close our eyes.' And you can hug me, which was not something she did add out loud.

Malachi lifted his arm and sat forward to slide away, while she was having trouble holding her head up. It was as if she'd been given a sedative, but she knew she'd been given a gift more precious than that. She'd been given the gift of sharing the load.

While she was still thinking about that, Malachi reached and took her hand. Pulled her gently to her feet, and before she could straighten he slid one strong arm under her knees and the other around her back and lifted her into his arms. He hugged her into his chest like some olden day knight carrying his princess to his tower.

She smiled sleepily up into his face. 'You're so strong,' she teased.

'Good to know all those hours in the gym weren't wasted,' he said seriously, and she snorted indelicately against his chest, his beautiful chest, and closed her eyes. Now this had to be a dream.

CHAPTER TWENTY-ONE

Malachi

LISANDRA IN HIS arms felt wonderful, so incredibly perfect that he couldn't help the way his fingers tightened. As he stared down into her face he saw the slight curl of her beautiful lips in a secret smile but her dark lashes hid her eyes. He could feel her relaxed and trusting as she lay against him, as she should be, because he would never hurt her.

He placed her gently on the opposite side of the bed to his and thought to himself how good she looked there. Too good.

She opened her eyes, eyes such a striking blue, those eyes like the ocean outside his window, and she smiled at him as he stepped away.

'There were two of us in this nap dream,' she said. 'Are you coming?'

'Very soon.' He stepped away from the

room to the pram and pushed it so that it stood beside the bed in full view, then opened the sliding wardrobe door behind him and pulled a thin summer blanket from the shelf. He floated half of it so that it covered her and sat on his side of the bed to remove his shoes and just his belt, so the metal wouldn't press against her.

Malachi eased down beside her and slid his arm under her shoulder, turning her gently away from him and pulling her back into his chest. 'Nap,' he said with a mock firmness, and her shoulders shook slightly in amusement. Though he couldn't see her face he knew she was smiling and he felt her relax even more against him.

Within a very short time they actually slept.

Malachi woke to a woman in his arms. Lisandra in his arms. It wasn't a dream.

On the negative she was fully dressed, and on the plus side, she lay relaxed in sleep. The scent of her hair and the skin at the back of her neck surrounded him in the most delicious way. Unconsciously his hand, the one spread under her breast, tightened to pull her closer.

In unconscious response her bottom snuggled in. There, he silently groaned, that whole positive-negative thing happening again. She was there but he couldn't have her.

So, this was what it was like? To care deeply for the person asleep in your arms. This ache to hold her like this for ever. To wake every morning with Lisandra, soft and warm, and that warmth not just physical but emotionally wonderful, all around him.

If only he were a better man.

If only he could be a better father than the man who had been so disappointed and derogatory towards him.

If only...

She stretched against him and he forced himself to let her go, watched her ease sideways and then turn on her back and roll to face him. 'I wonder if this is the first time in the last weeks that I've woken on my own without the boys pressing my alarm.'

His sense of humour, one that seemed to grow and mature when he was around Lisandra, sparked. 'Did I press you with my alarm?'

She made that delightful snort that she'd made when he'd carried her across to the bed. He could see her teeth in this smile and it made his own mouth widen.

'Malachi,' she said, 'you are one of a kind.'

'Back at you, Miss Calhoun,' he murmured as he leaned forward and kissed her.

CHAPTER TWENTY-TWO

Lisandra

WAKING IN MALACHI's arms was like starting life all over again.

That might have been because she'd allowed herself to sleep so deeply for the first time since the twins were born that she felt renewed, just by trusting that he would hear them if she didn't. Or because Malachi's arms felt so wonderful. His whole body had felt wonderful spooned against hers. Probably, that feeling of renewal came from all of the above.

When she rolled to look at him he was watching her with his hazel eyes so dark, such smouldering bedroom dark, and if she hadn't already felt his body's reaction to her against her bottom she would have seen it in his eyes.

She stared into a wondrous world she'd thought lost for ever and knew that in the short time that she'd known Malachi Madden he had grown to mean so much to her.

Strangely, she'd never had an issue with their difference in circumstance—he was ridiculously wealthy and she was…not poor, but only adequately funded—and she'd always intended to thank him for his generosity and leave.

All that had changed now because she didn't want to leave him. She wanted to lie like this, in this bed, every night, every morning, and most certainly for naps like this during the day, with Malachi's arms around her.

His beautiful eyes grew darker and she knew the moment that he'd decided to kiss her. She felt her own lips part as she stared, suddenly breathless, into the depths of his intense gaze and watched his mouth come closer.

She'd wondered what it would be like to be kissed by Malachi…but nothing prepared her.

Then the thought was gone as he brushed her lips with his, nibbled gently at her lower lip, swept his hot and heavenly mouth backwards and forwards, backwards and forwards until she was leaning into him, hungry, desperately urging him to take her mouth.

When he sealed his lips against her the

sweep of his tongue opened her to him and she breathed him in.

Welcomed him, in fact, with all her being. The gentleness, then the unexpected authority and the sweeping reverence all combining to tumble any resistance she might have had. Not that she had much because she was lost. Swirled into a sensation of pleasure, hunger, desperation…and love.

The thought exploded into her mind like fireworks in the silent room. Malachi cared. Malachi loved her. But there was sadness and despair in this kiss because Malachi didn't believe in the future.

His passion and longing brought tears to her eyes because she tasted, inhaled, sensed profoundly the sadness at the back of this kiss and she drew him closer, deeper, wordlessly reassuring him, but the sadness remained. Why was he sad?

A baby cried and Malachi pulled away well before she would have and eased himself out of the bed.

Lisandra flopped onto her back and blew out a breath. So much for wondering if Malachi could kiss. The man was a kissing machine. A master smoocher. A maestro. And there was worry when she thought about that underlying sadness she couldn't deny she'd felt and wanted to assuage.

Malachi's sadness came from somewhere deep, she knew it wasn't something they could lightly discuss, but she'd think on it and take the insight that she'd gained today and the kindness that she knew he would still offer until they could work this out.

They had to work this out, because now she knew Malachi loved her and of a certainty, she loved him.

The thought sat comfortably. Yes, she loved the quirky, blunt, generous, kind man who kissed like an angel. A wickedly sensuous angel and she never, ever, wanted him to be sad. Or for him to be alone with that sadness.

Suddenly she remembered Simon's comment: 'You might have to do the running...' For what? Had a man who'd seen them together for less than an hour known something? Something neither she nor Malachi had seen? Had Simon guessed it would be like this?

Lisandra rose from the bed and crossed to where Malachi held Bennett to his chest, patting the small back with his big hands. She wanted to slide her own hands around his waist and comfort him from behind as he'd held her, but something told her he'd put up a wall and it wouldn't go well.

Instead, she bided her time. 'Here. I'll take him.' Took her son from his hands and crossed to the white lounge and opened her blouse to feed him.

'I'll make fresh tea,' Malachi said from behind her shoulder and she heard him walk away. The sounds of the jug switching on and then more sounds as Malachi disappeared into the bedroom where the door shut.

Why was he sad? she thought and stared down at the little face watching hers. 'Why is our Malachi sad?' she said softly and Bennett paused in his drinking and stared at her with wise eyes. 'You don't know why, either, do you, little man?' she said.

'Maybe it's all too fast for him? I'm overwhelming him?' She raised her brows at Bennett. 'Are we overwhelming him? Maybe we should all go back upstairs tonight and just leave the door open like we were supposed to. Take things more slowly?' And then she heard Bastian complain that he'd been left behind in the pram.

The bedroom door opened and she heard Malachi's voice. 'Missing out, are you, young man? I know where they went. I'll take you.'

When he came around the front of the

lounge carrying Bastian, she smiled at him. 'You're talking to babies.'

'I thought I heard you chatting away?'

He passed the boomerang pillow and she slipped Bennett onto it so she could make way for his brother on the other side. Then Malachi reached for her cold cup of tea and placed it on the tray next to the teapot. 'Earl Grey again or would you like something different?'

'You're spoiling me.'

'It's Sunday. I can.'

True. He worked a lot of the time. Except when he was with her. 'Then I'll have peppermint this time, please.'

CHAPTER TWENTY-THREE

Malachi

ON MONDAY MORNING, Malachi had to force himself to go out of his own door. He'd slipped up the stairs to the loft, something he'd done a few times since Lisandra had moved back upstairs last night, to say goodbye and ensure she needed nothing before he left.

Mrs Harris would be here in fifteen minutes, a good hour before she normally came, and Lisandra hadn't wanted him to wait and make himself late.

He hated leaving her with the boys alone after he'd promised her she wouldn't be solo for the next forty-eight hours. Yet here he was going down in the lift, and leaving them all behind.

How had his life changed so much in so short a time?

Yesterday's kiss had changed everything.

He should never have made that move but she'd been impossible to resist. The feel of Lisandra's mouth against his, her sweetness and warmth, the feeling of homecoming— such sensations and emotions he'd never had with any woman, and wanted to have with Lisandra for the rest of his life.

He'd wanted to wrap her up in his arms and never let her go, but he knew he'd been a fool to open up wants and needs he'd accepted long ago would never be his.

Not surprisingly, that kiss had sent Lisandra back upstairs to the loft and confirmed something he'd been afraid of. He wanted Lisandra Calhoun with every atom of his being but he wasn't good enough for her. Or for her boys. He never would be.

Her going back upstairs to sleep was a kindness on her part.

That was fine. If nothing changed between them now, then he had more in his life than he'd ever had and he should be grateful for that.

If she stayed living in the loft.

If he hadn't chased her away with his advances.

If he could rebuild the trust he'd smashed

down and reassure her friendship was all he wanted.

Because out of everything he wanted her and the boys to stay.

Ginny was waiting for him when he reached his office. 'How are they?' she asked before he could offer a good morning.

Dear Ginny. 'No problems. Mrs Harris is there early and I need to be out of here before five tonight so Lisandra has back-up for another twenty-four hours.'

'Got it.' Ginny agreed with a determined nod, followed by an inclination towards his inner sanctum. 'And Simon Purdy's in there waiting for you.'

'Why?' Had new results for Bastian come through that he hadn't seen yet. Had they found something that put the baby at risk? He should never have left Lisandra this morning.

'He didn't say.'

Ginny's voice broke into his sudden fear and Malachi strode towards his office. 'Hold my calls until I let you know, please.'

'Yes, I will.'

He glanced back at her. 'Except Lisandra, of course.' He patted his pocket. Thank goodness for mobile phones. In fact, since he'd met Lisandra, he held gratitude for the instrument that meant she could contact him at any time even if it was to leave a message.

Ginny murmured, lifting her hand to her face, 'Of course,' and he had a suspicion she was smiling behind her fingers. Smiling at what? There could be bad news. What was wrong with everybody at the moment?

He pushed the door wider. 'Simon. I didn't expect to see you this morning. Is something wrong with Bastian's results?'

His friend had been staring out of the office window at the ocean. 'No. Of course not. I would have phoned you. Still all good.' He waved back towards Ginny. 'I had to come over to see a baby in your NICU earlier and I thought I'd catch you before you started. You're always a hard man to track down through the day.'

Malachi's overwhelming relief made him gruff. 'What can I do for you, then?' Malachi glanced at his watch. He'd only do one ward round today instead of his usual two unless the midwives had a concern about one of his patients. That would get him home earlier.

'Offering advice.' Simon's voice seemed to come from far away as Malachi wondered if Mrs Harris had arrived yet. 'Hello. Malachi? What are you thinking about?' Simon's voice intruded into his thoughts.

'Sorry. Did you say something?' He ran his hand through his hair. Stared at his friend in exasperation. 'I'm trying to work out how I'm going to get home earlier tonight before my housekeeper leaves.'

Simon leant his big shoulder against the window frame. 'I've never seen you act this way. Ever. Not about a woman.'

He did not need to be an interesting specimen for his friend to watch. 'Well, now you've seen it, you can go.'

'Ah, man…' Simon shook his head as he pushed off the window frame. 'I just wondered if you needed a hand to work it out.'

As if anyone could help the way he was. 'What's there to work out? Lisandra's a dear friend, that's all, and one day, soon, she'll move out and find a good man to marry.'

'You are a good man. A great man. Ask her to marry you.'

Malachi pulled a face and stepped to his desk and swept up the sheet of paper waiting for him there. 'I mean one who'll be a decent father to her children.' He glared up at Simon, remembering yesterday. 'You and I will go on, just like you said, saving other people's families.'

Simon raised his hands. 'I'm sorry I said that. It's not true. You would love those boys.

I think you do already. No kid needs more than a father who loves them.' Simon added gently, 'And who loves their mother.'

'Not my forte.' Pain squeezed through him. He didn't believe that was all Lisandra's boys deserved.

More quietly, Simon said, 'I think you and Lisandra are perfect together.'

'Really?' For heaven's sake. The man was delusional. 'You deduced this from your ex- tended observation of us both?' he said dryly as he re-scanned today's theatre list, which wasn't sinking in. 'What was it? Three lots of ten minutes?'

'It didn't take long to see. Good grief, Mala- chi, even your grandmother approves.'

That made his head jerk up. 'What on earth makes you say that?'

'Because Millicent came in and hugged Lisandra yesterday when she checked on Bas- tion. I've never seen her hug anybody.'

Malachi stared. Blinked. Replayed it. 'My grandmother was in the paediatric intensive care? Yesterday?' And why was he the last to know? Then he remembered she'd phoned him in the middle of everything just after he'd left Lisandra on Sunday morning. 'She went into the public hospital?' One she hadn't been in since his grandfather had died there.

'She did.'

Now that, Malachi thought, was too much to think about and he needed to get moving.

He narrowed his eyes and stared at his friend. 'Why are you here, again?'

Simon huffed out a laugh and headed for the door. He turned and said over his shoulder, 'Because I think you could screw it up and I don't want that to happen.'

Simon shook his head at Malachi's confusion. 'Come see me if it all starts to go pear-shaped, okay? She cares about you, too.' Then his interfering friend walked away as if he hadn't thrown Malachi into total confusion.

He pushed it all away and re-examined the day's theatre list and his part in it, folded the sheet neatly, and slid it into his trouser pocket.

He was still confused about Simon's visit as he stopped at Ginny's desk. 'Please see if you can reschedule the last appointment for today and tomorrow,' he asked.

'I've already done that. Unless we're really stuck, I'll be trying for it most days.'

'Oh. Thank you.' That was a good idea. He headed for the door but stopped before he stepped into the corridor. 'Thanks for coming in yesterday, Ginny. Lisandra said you helped a lot.'

'You're both welcome,' Ginny said. 'Ward

Three asked if you could stop in there, first on your rounds, this morning.'

He nodded and started his day.

CHAPTER TWENTY-FOUR

Lisandra

LISANDRA WATCHED MALACHI disappear down the stairs and a minute later she heard the door close gently in his apartment.

Earlier, with the loft door open between their previously separate living spaces, it had been strange to hear all the daily minutiae of Malachi's life in his apartment downstairs.

Strange and reassuring. It was also funny how she could imagine what he was doing a lot of the time.

Then again, since she'd moved back here last night, he had reappeared in her unit so many times to check she didn't need him that she might as well have stayed down there.

She knew what she needed to take her stress away. Malachi's arms around her. In fact, she was having the devil of a time to stop thinking about his mouth on hers and how much more she wanted him holding her in his embrace.

She was in love with Malachi Madden.

She blew out a breath. That had come out of the blue. And with more force and substance than she could believe possible.

Guilt slammed into her and she winced.

What about Richard?

It was not even a year since he'd been taken from her and she'd found another man? Loved another man? Already?

They were so different, the two men she'd loved, but what she felt for Malachi didn't lessen the past she still held in a special corner of her heart.

Which reminded her. It was time to text another photo to Richard's mother. She didn't know whether to tell her about Bastian's scare or not—but decided it could be something that could wait if they ever had a chance to talk. The last thing she wanted to do was exacerbate their grief for their son.

She'd had several short but promising texts in the last weeks from Richard's mother. It seemed Josie was making headway with Clint because of the likeness of the boys to Richard when he was a baby.

Josie had taken a phone snap of Richard's

baby photo and shared it with Lisandra, who could see the resemblance as well. It made her feel her sons were more of a part of their father's estranged family. Maybe one day, maybe even with Malachi by her side, she would be asked to visit them again.

She would always be thankful for Richard and for the gift of his sons, boys she now hoped would truly become Malachi's sons. She would ensure her boys knew they'd been blessed with two wonderful fathers.

But today was a day to look to the future.

A day to drop the guilt, the blame, the denial of something incredibly special that had grown out of loss and grief and new life and new friendship.

Malachi was a wonderful man and she had forgiven herself for unexpectedly moving on from the past. Had decided there was no right length of time to grieve—be it one year, one decade, a lifetime, all could be right—but it also had to be right to hold gratitude for the unexpected gift of not being alone and for being so selflessly loved by Malachi.

Today she'd say goodbye to Richard and she would fight for Malachi.

She glanced at the aquamarine expanse outside the window and thought of the man she'd fallen in love with.

It wasn't a blind infatuation, like the crazy, consuming attraction that she suspected she might have had with Richard. This was a warts-and-all awareness. Malachi wasn't perfect and neither was she, and they both brought baggage. But she had been gifted the opportunity to unfurl a relationship with an amazing man. Hopefully, whatever was holding Malachi back would resolve enough for them to be able to find the solution to their barriers. She needed to find Malachi's fears and help him face them.

She suspected from what he'd said about marriage and not having children—which was ridiculous with the way he handled the boys—that his hang-ups had to do with his father. Millicent had said something along those lines as well.

Was Malachi's grandmother the answer?

Millicent. Millicent, who had visited her yesterday in the hospital and had looked unexpectedly shattered at Bastian's close shave with death.

Millicent, who had shared her private mobile number and had said she could ring her any time.

Today?

Lisandra knew Malachi's grandmother to be an early riser because she'd been immaculate and early on that first Saturday morning when she'd met her. Let's hope that went for today as well.

An hour later, once she'd showered, dressed, and the boys were back asleep, Lisandra pressed the number for Malachi's grandmother.

'Who is this?' Crisp and curt.

'Millicent. It's Lisandra. I hope you don't mind that I called. I just wanted to say thank you for visiting us at the hospital, yesterday.'

'Lisandra.' Instant change in tone. Phew. 'I'm so pleased you rang. How is dear Bastian this morning? And Bennett, of course.' There was genuine concern, interest and, if she wasn't mistaken, pleasure that Lisandra had called. Some of the tension left her shoulders.

It did feel good to talk to Malachi's grandmother. This was what she'd hoped for from Richard's mother. She suspected her own sad little need was to search for a replacement for the mother and grandmother she had lost.

'Lisandra? Are you there?'

'Sorry. I went vague for a moment. Both boys have been perfect gentlemen since they arrived home yesterday.' She couldn't help her glance at the open door to the stairwell.

'Malachi insisted we leave the loft door open because Dr Purdy wanted me to have access to assistance for the next forty-eight hours.'

'What an excellent idea. So is Malachi there?'

She wished. 'No. He's gone to work but Mrs Harris has arrived an hour early and will stay until he comes home tonight. It's just for the next twenty-four hours.'

'Oh.' Did that sound like disappointment? 'That must be reassuring for you.'

'It is.' There was a pause, she felt her bravery ebb, and Lisandra winced and almost chickened out. She couldn't chicken out of loving Malachi. No. At the thought, she straightened her shoulders. 'I wondered if you'd be interested in having lunch with me today. If you're not busy, of course.

There was a small pause and Lisandra's heart sank but before it could make it all the way to her toenails, Millicent said, 'I'm free. I'd enjoy that. Thank you for thinking of me.' She sounded sincerely pleased, and Lisandra let out a sigh of relief. Malachi's grandmother went on, 'What would you like me to bring?'

Yourself, your knowledge of Malachi, your understanding, Lisandra thought. 'I have a full freezer and I did see a lovely gourmet quiche in there that I could easily slip into the oven. I'll make a green salad to go with it and we can drink tea.'

'Perfect. What time? And which apartment?' Amusement sounded in the question. Was Millicent teasing her?

She suspected she was and smiled. 'Twelve. And the loft. But if you end up through the wrong door I'm just up the stairs.'

Millicent laughed. 'Clever girl. I'll see you then.'

When Millicent knocked on the door of the loft she brought two non-alcoholic bottles of apple cider and a tray of pastries. Lisandra gestured her in. 'Welcome to my eyrie.'

'Thank you, I'm delighted you invited me. Where are the boys?'

'Asleep.' She pushed wider the crack of the door to the boy's bedroom and two little bodies lay quietly in their portable cots.

'Angels.'

'Most times,' Lisandra murmured, and the two women smiled at each other. 'I've set places at the small table on the balcony and there's a shade sail attached to the wall to keep us out of the sun.'

She'd already set the heated quiche and green salad out there under a muslin throw, expecting Millicent to be punctual. She had been. To the minute. No surprises. Which was nice.

Lisandra brought one of the bottles of apple cider and two glasses and gestured Millicent to the best seat with the clearest view out over the ocean. She stood over the glasses and poured the gold sparkling liquid.

Millicent sighed happily. 'It really is a glorious outlook.'

Lisandra eased into her own chair and breathed in the salt and the sunshine and the new aroma of apple cider and quiche.

Millicent glanced down at the visible edge of Malachi's pool that she could see. 'Have you been in the pool?'

'Lord, no.' She laughed. 'I haven't had time to have a long shower, let alone cavort in the water.'

'Pity.'

Lisandra waved that away. 'I told Malachi I wouldn't be swanning past him to use his pool.'

Millicent raised her perfect brows. Dryly she said, 'I think he might enjoy that.'

Lisandra wasn't sure what to say to that and she wasn't quite relaxed enough with her visitor to be where she wanted before she dived into the personal.

Instead of answering she began to serve the

quiche and passed Millicent the salad. The next few minutes were taken up with eating.

'Since the boys arrived it has been busy,' she said a few minutes later.

'And when do you think it'll all settle down?'

'Apart from yesterday's horror, it's getting better every day now. Since the boys passed the six-week mark. I'm starting to feel human and they don't wake me at night as much because I feed them so often through the day.'

'It seems to be working for you. Malachi did mention he helps with bath times when he's available. It seems so out of character.'

And this was what she wanted to know. 'Why is it out of character? He has a job that involves babies.'

Millicent put down her glass of cider very carefully. 'Don't get me wrong. I'm delighted. But he's always said he wasn't father material. I'm hoping the experience he's gaining from you and the boys will change his mind for the future.'

So was she. The near future. 'He's very good with them. And it's amusing how skilled he's become at encouraging wriggling feet into the small playsuits.'

Millicent sent her an approving smile. 'I love how he's grown being around you.'

The kind remark made Lisandra's cheeks warm and inside a little more of the cold part of her thawed. 'That's lovely of you to say. He is wonderful.'

Millicent lifted her head. Held Lisandra's gaze with hazel eyes a very similar colour to her grandson's. 'And can you see a future with you and Malachi?'

Lisandra shouldn't have been surprised that his grandmother had put it out there. After all, that was why she'd asked Millicent to come. To sound her out. Listen. And ask advice.

She sat back in her chair. 'No mincing words for you, is there, Millicent?'

Those perfect brows rose again. 'I'm eighty-four years old, my dear. No time to pussyfoot around if I want to see Malachi happy before I die.'

'And you think he'd be happy with me.'

'I believe so. It's early days, I know, but I think you're fond of him. Do you think you could love him?'

'Easily. The man is everything I'd want for myself and for my boys. He's wonderful company and I miss him when he's not here. As for love, it's too late already. But I'm wary there's a reason he's holding back and I don't want to push him, hurt him, or make him unhappy. He's been so kind.'

Millicent sat back with a big breath of relief. 'Thank the stars. And yes, Malachi has always been kind. So, you asked me here to find out why he's pulling back?'

It was truth time all right. 'To help me understand why,' she clarified. 'I'm thinking it had something to do with his father because, as you say, Malachi told me he would never marry and never have children. Yet, I see him exhibiting all the wonderful traits anybody could possibly wish for in a parent or husband.'

'History.' Millicent sighed. 'All tragic history. My daughter, Malachi's mother, was always impetuous, full of life but blind when she married an impossible man. And when she left him, as she had to for her own mental health, she was not permitted to take Malachi. He threatened her with the courts if she tried.'

'That's horrible.'

'It was. Who knows what would have happened if they'd both had time to cool down? But she drove away recklessly and an accident killed her.'

Millicent's eyes drifted to the ocean and she sighed. When she looked back sadness seemed wrapped around her like a dark cloud. 'Malachi's childhood changed in an instant, ignored and despised by a man who should have seen his son's worth, and dished a cold and lonely upbringing without the mother who loved him.'

When she lifted her chin her eyes glinted with unshed tears. 'His father changed that night into a dreadful man who ridiculed Malachi's kindness and undermined his son's confidence at every turn. The boy couldn't do anything right and when I offered to raise him myself to protect him, I was practically banished as well.'

'That's even worse than I imagined.' Lisandra had guessed it had not been an easy childhood, but this was crueller than she'd suspected. Poor Malachi. Poor Millicent. Poor Millicent's daughter.

'Thankfully, his father sent him to boarding school when he turned twelve. At least I could get to take him home for the weekends. Malachi was determined to do well and become a doctor. We grew close.'

'I can see that.' Lisandra touched the other woman's hand briefly. 'His voice softens when he speaks about you.'

Millicent searched her face as if she didn't believe it, but the truth was there to see. 'Thank you. I wonder sometimes.'

'Don't. He adores you.'

'And I believe he adores you.' Millicent sat

back, her face serious. 'So, what are we going to do about that?'

Lisandra understood, a lot more anyway. She had clarity now and a mission. 'I'm going to show him I love and believe in him. The rest is up to him.'

CHAPTER TWENTY-FIVE

Malachi

MALACHI MADE IT back up the lift with ten minutes to spare before five p.m. He let himself in through his apartment, thanked Mrs Harris, who smiled and waved her hand from the kitchen where she was stirring something that smelled delicious.

'Thank you for staying,' he said.

'I've had a lovely day. The table's set and there's a mild chicken curry and rice, with some papadums, if you'd like to share it with Lisandra. My special recipe.'

He wondered if curry would upset the twins, but she must have read his mind.

'She said it would be fine with the wee ones if it was mild.'

He smiled. She'd never made him a meal but he'd take it with pleasure. He'd been so intent on getting back in time he hadn't thought about the evening meal. 'Thank you, Mrs Harris. That sounds wonderful.' His stomach rumbled and he remembered he hadn't stopped for lunch.

Mrs Harris turned the stove off and departed, promising to be early tomorrow.

He put down his briefcase and did what he'd wanted to do all day. He climbed the stairs to the loft. The door stood open, of course, but still he knocked.

Lisandra sat relaxed on the lounge, a place he'd seen her so many times, with a sleepy baby over each shoulder and a big, beautiful smile that came his way like a sunbeam that warmed his whole world.

His Lisandra, his Mother Earth and lovely 'tenant', he reminded himself, that he didn't want to lose. He thought about Simon saying not to screw it up, but he had no idea where to go from here. The dreaded awkwardness crept over him like a sticky web.

'How was your day?' he asked and reached down to take Bennett from her and slide him up over his own shoulder.

'Wonderful. Mrs Harris was a doll, and we've already bathed the babies, so my day has been very smooth and social.' She leaned her cheek against the little body near her ear. 'How was yours?'

'Not quite as smooth but I did manage to make it home in time.'

She raised amused brows at his slightly stressed reply. 'Did you have time for lunch?'

He smiled at her insight. 'No. Did you?'

'Your grandmother came and we had quiche on the balcony. It was very pleasant.'

He blinked. 'Did she invite herself again?' He'd have to lay down some rules.

'No. I phoned her. She gave me her number yesterday when she came to see Bastian at the hospital.'

He'd been going to ask about that. 'Simon said he'd seen her there.'

She straightened and brought Bastian closer to her chest in a protective hug. 'Yes, she said once she'd heard the news she'd had to come. What else did Simon say? Were there any other results from the tests? Did he find something?'

'No.' He sat down next to her so that their legs touched and he hoped pushing their bodies together would give her comfort. It was instinctual and he felt her relax beside him. He held her gaze. 'Everything is fine.

'As for Simon, he came to give me a pep talk about something else.' Anxious to reassure her but, after it was out, he could have bitten the words back. He hurried on. 'All the formal test results are in and nothing was flagged. I have them on my computer and we can pore over them together when you're ready.'

Sadly, she wasn't diverted. 'What was the pep talk about?'

Not something he wanted to share like this. 'What was your talk with my grandmother about?'

She smiled at him. 'Possibly the same thing?'

He blinked. She stood up and carried Bastian to the bedroom and almost immediately she was back and took Bennett from him. 'The boys are going to bed and the adults are having a conversation.'

He sat back. An unwilling smile tugging on his lips. Lisandra didn't do awkward, and he felt the strands of unease unravel. She returned and sat beside him. Close. Incredibly close. Wonderfully close.

She even took his hand, and hers felt warm yet fragile in his, until she turned to stare into his eyes, the blue of her gaze dazzling him.

'Malachi, I've been very happy here.'

'Good.' But past tense? He wasn't sure where this was leading but he had a sinking feeling he wasn't going to like it.

She ignored his interruption. 'I've loved every minute of getting to know you, and that's for me—not just because you're a delight with the babies.' Her eyes searched his as if she needed him to hear and agree with her. 'I think you're fabulous with them. But you're also fabulous with me.'

Oh, God. She was leaving, he thought. His world came to a shuddering halt. He had to stop her. 'You don't have to go.'

She squeezed his hand. 'I don't want to go.'

He put his other over the top as if to stop her from leaving him. 'Then don't.'

Softly, he heard the words he'd dreaded, 'I can't just stay here for ever as your tenant.'

Yes, she could. Of course she could. Ridiculously, his brain screamed, he could leave if that would make it easier for her. 'Why not?'

She pulled free and sat back widening the distance between them. Raised her brow in amusement. 'When you get married your wife wouldn't be happy.'

Now that wasn't a problem. 'I'm not getting married.'

She watched his face intently. 'My turn to ask why not?'

He shrugged, the awkwardness creeping back. 'I'm not husband material.'

She widened her eyes. Gently poked him in the chest with one finger. Said very slowly, 'I think you're perfect husband material.'

He blinked. She did? 'You do?' That was unexpected. And bore thinking about. He looked towards the room where the boys lay. He certainly wasn't father material. No doubt there.

'And you are wonderful with the boys. I couldn't wish for more care.'

She leaned into him and whispered in his ear, 'And you're an amazing kisser.'

His heart began to pound and Malachi reached down and took her fingers back in his. The awkwardness had disappeared in an instant. 'I am, am I?' He shifted closer and made up that distance she'd created.

'Oh, yes. Best ever. Super.' She nodded solemnly but he could see her eyes sparkling with mischief. Blue pools daring him to fight for her.

He was being herded, he knew that, but it wasn't awkward, it was a challenge and suddenly he was very keen on getting in on the action. 'You're pretty darn hot yourself,' he said, and slid his arm around the delightful waist he adored, pulling her into his side.

'The dilemma is,' she said softly, 'I don't want to hurt you by staying if you can't see a future with us all.'

Oh, he could see it. Dream it. He just believed she deserved more. 'I can see one day you'll leave and find someone to be there for you instead of me. But until then,' he said, the words scratching and scoring his heart as they left his mouth, 'until then you could stay.'

Her face drew closer and she whispered as her mouth brushed against his, 'Why would I possibly want anyone else but you?'

And the penny dropped.

CHAPTER TWENTY-SIX

Lisandra

SHE FELT THE moment he realised she wanted him. As she had no doubt he wanted her. His shock, and delight and what felt like possessiveness in the tenseness of his body as he moved even closer. *Oh, Malachi, you adorable man,* she mentally sighed in relief as his lips pressed against hers and his hand slid firmly behind her neck to hold her there.

He took over the kiss, deeper, stronger, like steel-covered velvet and fire…my stars, this man could kiss.

She closed her eyes and sank into the swirling wonder of Malachi's mouth, felt the tension slide from her shoulders, her belly warming, and a smile growing at the corners of her mouth.

They surfaced, and with his mouth still sliding across her lips he murmured, 'So you'd like to stay here? For ever?' His mouth brushing hers and a smile in his voice.

'I'd prefer to move down to your bedroom.'

He made a noise deep and low and in assent. 'Oh, yes. Great idea. Asap. Later on, when the boys are older, they could live upstairs and we'd have more privacy than we knew what to do with.'

'Unless we filled the other rooms with children as well.'

He pulled away. 'You'd consider having more children? With me?'

'If we were blessed…then I can't wait.'

'What if I'm a terrible father?'

And there it was. His deep-seated lack of confidence that was so unfounded. 'How can you be? You're already a wonderful dad to the B twins.' She watched him blink at the word dad. It made her throat tighten and ache for all the years he'd doubted himself.

He turned his face. Looked out of the window. Hiding his eyes. 'That's just luck with babies. I don't know how to be a real father.'

'Let me help you understand.' She took both his cheeks in her hands, turned him, and stared into his face. 'The starting and ending point is love. If you can love…' She looked and could see the love in his eyes—love for her, love for the children in the next room—

how could he not see how amazing he would be? 'Anything is possible.'

'You deserve more.'

How to convince him? She hitched up her courage and dared to dream. 'Do you love me?'

'With all my heart.' No hesitation. Straight out. The words brought tears to her eyes.

She gestured to the room that held the boys. 'Do you love my sons?'

He blew out his breath softly. Nodded. Smiled. His eyes twinkled. 'I do.'

'Then you will be a wonderful father. A wise woman I know once said, "All children need is someone to love them, someone to take responsibility, and someone to provide a safe place for them to grow." Together, we can provide all of that.'

He almost looked convinced—but not quite. And she knew what it was. His big fear. 'What about the demands of my work?'

And that was his dear blindness that she loved so much. 'You will always give your best to your patients. It's not in you to do anything else. And I love you for that.'

She saw his eyes widen but there was more to say before they dwelt on her feelings. 'Who has managed to help me bath the boys more than fifty per cent of the time in the last few weeks?'

He looked thoughtful and she smiled. 'Already, you've prioritised your work hours. Managed to spend less time at the hospital without causing harm to your patients. Maybe you can even see that having enough rest actually makes you a better doctor when you are working.'

'Hmm.' Non-committal but he was listening—and, she hoped, hearing her. Because she understood his ethic.

'Because you love us, you can stay up with a sick baby when you've already done a ten-hour work day. Could stay up for me.' And there was double entendre there.

His eyes gleamed and then dulled. 'I have call. I'll always have call. What if you get fed up?'

'Yes. You have call. But not every night. You might not be able to watch them play cricket every Saturday, like some other dads, but you'll watch them when you can. You could read a story another day, and cook dinner another. Even if you're still working long hours, it's the cumulation of little things that make a good father, it's having someone who's got their back, who's there for their mother, even if not always able to be present every minute of every day—no parent can be, and it would be very unhealthy to be there all the time anyway!'

She watched the hope brighten his eyes. Saw him lift his head as he stared at her. As if she were promising him the world and not a jam-packed life full of kids and drama and scattered homelife.

He leaned his forehead against hers and she heard the breath he drew in. 'Are you sure?'

'Absolutely. If you'll have me. And my boys.'

'Please may I have you? And your boys. I can't imagine my home if you weren't here. If I lost you all I would be alone again and for the first time in a very long time I want to come home. To you. To our boys.' He shook his head. Breathed out the words, 'I'll have a family.'

She stroked his hair. 'You are my family. We are yours.'

His eyes searched hers. Serious. Intent. 'Will you marry me, Lisandra?'

Oh, Malachi, she thought. *How can I be so lucky?* 'I love you. I'd love to.'

His mouth brushed hers and he whispered against her lips. 'When?'

'Soon.'

'How soon?'

'Let's not have a total rush into this. You have to really live with us yet. Get used to the craziness that is my life.'

He considered that. She saw it in his thoughtful gaze. That he could see she wouldn't budge. Tried his own ultimatum. 'When the boys are six months old.'

'If we haven't driven you mad by then.'

He sat back. 'Do I have to wait that long for you to move downstairs?' Disappointment clear and she wanted to hug him.

'No. We can do that much earlier.'

'When?' His eyes were laughing at her, and full of love.

'Now.'

'Excellent.'

Four months later, the wedding

Malachi stood at the leafy edge of the Tweed River in golden afternoon light. In front of him stood a metal border shaped like a heart and full of flowers. The elaborate gold and cream blooms that his grandmother had organised were elegant and stylish as they twisted to shape a frame for the sharing of the vows.

Behind him the wide lawns were immaculate, the riverfront restaurant shone like a fairyland, and even Malachi had to admit the wedding centre felt a fitting place to celebrate their marriage.

Except his bride wasn't beside him, Simon was, and, as much as he enjoyed his friend's company, he really wanted Lisandra.

He'd been trying desperately to ignore the fifty people sitting on white chairs under the trees each side of the gold carpet that led to where he stood. He'd never been a person who enjoyed the limelight, but his grandmother had said this was as few guests as he could possibly have.

His bride-to-be had smiled at Millicent's insistence and laughingly agreed, and he had to admit he smiled every time he thought of the genuine warmth between the two women in his life.

As for the wedding—he just wished they'd get to the part where he could kiss the bride.

The music changed to the entrance waltz, thank the stars for that, he thought as he turned eagerly to follow the golden road to find a glimpse of the woman he loved.

Instead, Ginny floated down the carpet in some silky, very flattering gold dress, pushing the pram with the two boys in matching suits to his. His grandmother had had the tiny suits made, which he thought ridiculous for babies six months old, but Lisandra had agreed, so he had too.

Bastian was scowling, something he seemed to enjoy, and Bennett looked extremely interested in the many faces they passed.

Ginny came to a stop a little to his right, manoeuvred the pram so the page boys were sitting up to look at the congregation, and then the music swelled.

Ahh, there she was. His eyes misted for a moment, grew intensely focussed as his Lisandra, his love, his beautiful wife-to-be met his eyes and smiled with all the love he still couldn't believe she gifted him.

She stood tall, slim like a reed, her beautiful ivory gown showing glimpses of her tanned shoulders as it fell past her long legs to sweep the carpet and splay out behind her.

She floated towards him. The deep sleeves hung like bells over her hands and the bouquet of gold and bronze flowers highlighted her blonde hair as it floated free under the veil he was so desperate to lift. Malachi's heart seemed to swell in his chest as he watched her come to him. He so adored her.

* * *

Lisandra gazed down the golden length of the carpet to the man of her dreams. Malachi Madden had changed her life, had shown her kindness and generosity she'd never seen before, but most of all his selfless love had made her melt with matching joy. His eyes, his beautiful hazel eyes, cherished her, and she stepped faster as she closed the distance between them.

Unconsciously, regardless of the protocol, he stepped towards her, his hand lifted and turned to take hers as if he couldn't wait to clasp them together.

'My love,' he breathed, and she felt his long fingers close over hers. He lifted her hand to his lips and kissed her knuckles.

Together they turned and closed the distance to the celebrant, who smiled at them. Finally, the time-worn words began to flow softly like a breeze around them and two little boys cooed in their pram.

When the vows were made and Malachi had thoroughly kissed the bride, they stood together in front of the small crowd. The applause rose and her cheeks warmed. Malachi's hand was tight over hers, and she felt as if her heart would burst with happiness as they walked the length of the carpet to greet their well-wishers.

'You got the girl, Malachi,' his friend said.

'Your turn now, Simon,' Malachi replied as he shook his best man's hand.

* * * * *

If you enjoyed this story, check out these other great reads from Fiona McArthur

Taking a Chance on the Best Man
Second Chance in Barcelona
The Midwife's Secret Child
Healed by the Midwife's Kiss

All available now!